ABOUT THIS BOOK

Welcome to Havenwood Falls, home to sexy men, strong women, and neighbors who bite. Discover supernatural mystery, thrills, and romance in a place where everyone has a deep, dark, and often deadly secret. This is only but one...

Two years ago, Kaela Peters nearly killed her fiancé by ripping his throat out. Once she gained control over her vampire urges, she hoped to rekindle their love, only to find him on one knee again—now with her best friend. She can't blame them for their betrayal, though. They've been compelled to forget that she even existed. But she can't forget them, so when she receives an unexpected job offer far away in the Colorado mountains, she seizes the opportunity to escape her past and the painful memories.

If only she'd known she was running right into her true past and memories that cut even deeper.

Her real name isn't Kaela Peters, Havenwood Falls and her new job are not what they seem on the surface, and the love of her life isn't the ex in Atlanta. As she starts piecing together the fragmented memories of her past and her moroi heritage, the passion of old love reignites. Until she discovers that the triggering of her vampire gene may have been foul play with dire consequences—and Xandru Roca, the epic love she'd left behind, has something to do with it all.

FORGET YOU NOT

A HAVENWOOD FALLS NOVELLA

KRISTIE COOK

HAVENWOOD FALLS BOOKS

Forget You Not by Kristie Cook

Old Wounds by Susan Burdorf

Fate, Love & Loyalty by E.J. Fechenda

The Winged & the Wicked by T.V. Hahn & Kristie Cook

Alpha's Queen by Lila Felix

Ink & Fire by R.K. Ryals

Lose You Not by Kristie Cook

Tragic Ink by Heather Hildenbrand

Nowhere to Hide by Belinda Boring

Flames Among the Frost by Amy Hale

Rock Me Gently by Susan Burdorf

From the Embers by Amy Miles

Defying Gravity by Kallie Ross

Break Me Not by Kristie Cook

How the Dead Lie by Stacey Rourke

The Lurkers Within by Danielle Bannister

The Collector: Awakening by Kristie Cook, R.K. Ryals, Belinda Boring & Nadirah Foxx

Addicted to You by Belinda Boring

Affliction Mine by C.J. Pinard

The Ward & the Wanderers by T.V. Hahn

Toil & Trouble by Melissa Wright

Of Salt and Stars by Seven Jane

Redefined by Morgan Wylie

Betrayal Among the Frost by Amy Hale

Forever Loyal by E.J. Fechenda

Fate's Demand by Emily Cyr

The Wu & the Wand by T.V. Hahn

A Demon's Redemption by JD Nelson

Also try the YA line, Havenwood Falls High; the historical paranormal line, Legends of Havenwood Falls; the darker, sexier side of town, Havenwood Falls Sin & Silk; and the local supernatural college, Sun & Moon Academy.

Stay up to date at www.HavenwoodFalls.com

BOOKS BY KRISTIE COOK

Sun & Moon Academy Book Two: Fall Semester

The Winged & the Wicked (with T.V. Hahn)

Havenwood Falls Short Story Anthology 2018

Havenwood Falls Short Story Anthology 2019

Havenwood Falls Short Story Anthology 2020

Havenwood Falls Short Story Anthology 2021

Havenwood Falls Spring Anthology 2022

Havenwood Falls Sunset Anthology 2022

BOOK OF PHOENIX

The Space Between

The Space Beyond

The Space Within

For those who never gave up on me, who supported me, who believed in me

And to the authors who have put their trust in me

It's wonderful to be back. Back among the mountains that remind us of our vulnerability, our ultimate lack of control over the world we live in. Mountains that demand humility, and yield so much peace in return.

~ Alex Lowe

CHAPTER 1

Nothing screamed badass vampire chick more than hiding behind a menu while your ex-fiancé and former best friend sucked each other's faces three tables over and five booths down. I could hear their lips smacking and smell their horn-dog pheromones from my small table at the back of the restaurant. As if hiding wasn't pathetic enough, I couldn't stop stealing glances at them from over the top of the laminated cardboard in my hands, some sick part of me reveling in the painful twists of my heart and knots in my gut. *That's supposed to be me.* My eyes squeezed shut to suppress the threatening tears as I slid further down in my seat.

Ugh. I'm such a freakin' masochist.

"Kaela Peters, you are such a fucking masochist."

My eyes popped open at the sound of my roommate's raspy voice to find the redhead plopping down in the chair across from me, her green apron bunched up in one hand. One of her brows lifted as she stared at me with big, blue eyes, gnawing on her plump bottom lip, painted as scarlet as her hair. The color was all the more vibrant against her unnaturally porcelain-white skin. Sindi was also a vampire; in fact, in a much more traditional way than I was. Her coloring, for example—pale like vampires should be while my skin was still the olive tone it had always been. Her eyes had stayed the same, except when she fed from the vein, and then they sort of glowed, but mine made a permanent change from brown to a greenish-gray when I turned. We hadn't figured that one out.

After enduring several long moments of her glare, I finally shrugged and widened my eyes with as much innocence as I could muster. "What? It's not like I followed them here."

"Not this time."

My eyes began to drift over to the happy couple once more before I snapped them back to her. I didn't fool her, though. She noticed, if rolling her eyes was any indication.

"I guess you're at least taking my advice," she muttered as she unfolded her long legs and stood to tie her apron around her small waist. "But when the hell were you going to tell me?"

My brows pinched together at the sudden change in her tone, from snarky to ... pained. It took a lot to hurt Sindi's feelings—her heart was possibly tougher than her indestructible body. Another of the differences between us. My body could heal itself in a short time; hers healed immediately. My skin burnt and blistered in the sun, but she'd burst into flames. I still needed oxygen (though not as much as a human), and she didn't. My heart still beat, while hers was silent. But could it still be broken? What could I have done to do so?

"I'm sorry," I said, "but tell you what?"

She blew out a quick breath. "It's okay, Kaela, I get it. When you joked about moving far away from here and your past, I was serious when I said you should. I'll miss you, but it's what you need. But don't lie to me about it."

"I really have no idea what you're talking about." Actually, muttering about moving away hadn't really been a joke, but not something I'd done anything about. Yet. My eyes stole another glimpse of the cuddling exes at the thought of leaving, and I sighed. I really was too much of a masochist.

Sindi's hands landed at her waist, and her long fingers tapped against her hip bones as she let out another huff. "Whisper Falls Inn? Job offer? You left the email open on your laptop this morning. How could you not even tell me that you'd applied? And Colorado? Really, Kaela? Do you know how long that drive from Atlanta would be? I can only drive at night! You couldn't find anything closer?"

I stared at her, confused. "Why wouldn't you fly?"

She rolled her eyes. "You know why."

I opened my mouth to ask because I had no idea why, but then shook my head. How she got to Colorado didn't matter.

"Unbunch your panties," I said instead. "I can't have a job offer. I haven't applied for anything new in ages. And definitely not in Colorado."

She glared at me for another long moment, and she must have seen the truth in my eyes because her baby blues began to soften and she started fiddling with the contents of her apron pocket. "Yeah, well, you shouldn't leave your shit out and open if you don't want me to know. But if you care at all about my opinion, I think it's pretty perfect for you. You should take it." She broke our eye contact as she glanced around the restaurant. "My shift's about to start. Where are you tonight?"

"Nowhere. I have the rare night off."

"Then get your ass home, and if you don't take that job, find another—a real one."

"Hey! You bartend and wait, too. You can't get any more real than those."

"*Those*. Multiple. When was your last day off? Three weeks ago? You really want to hold down two jobs for the rest of your very long life? And at a 24-hour, hole-in-the-wall diner and meat-market nightclub? You're too smart for this, Kae. Go use your degree, for Christ's sake." She turned and headed for the kitchen.

"Yeah, well, easier said than done. Not too many companies have night shifts for their PR teams."

I stood up and threw some money on the table, although I hadn't eaten anything. I *could* eat food. Blood sustained me, but I still loved food. Just not while watching the Ryan & Heather Sappy Love Show starring the two people who'd been my favorite souls in the world at one time. They still kind of were. Sindi had nudged them into second and third place, but I still loved them both. It wasn't their fault they'd fallen for each other. That was all on me.

"Sindi," I called out to her back as she retreated. She turned halfway and threw me an impatient look. It was all a cover, I knew. She'd never tell me I was one of *her* favorite people—she'd never open up enough to admit to that anyone—but she'd basically just shown it. "I'm not going anywhere. Relax."

"Don't worry about me, doll face. You do what you need to do. I will be fine. Always am." Her mouth curved up in a smirk before she tossed her red ponytail over her shoulder and disappeared between the swinging doors to the kitchen.

I headed down the corridor toward the bathrooms—and the back door. Although I hadn't permanently left the area in the two years since the night that changed my entire life, I'd been successful in avoiding running into *them*, and I didn't want to change that now. I might have sometimes (frequently) watched (stalked) from a distance, but the thought of actually coming anywhere close to Ryan or Heather sent me into panic mode. Sindi had compelled them both to forget me and everything that had happened between us, but unfortunately her vampire power didn't work on me, fellow vampire and all. I remembered it all—the good, the bad, and the very gruesome ugly.

The cool night air of winter in the South was a welcome relief as I slipped into the dark alley and headed home, thinking about how Sindi had been my saving grace when I'd been a newborn vampire. She'd found me in this very alley covered in blood. My fiancé's blood. Hence, the "ex" part of our relationship. I'd nearly killed him when I ripped half his throat out. Hey, I didn't know what I was doing. Seriously. We'd gone to sleep after making love, and I awoke a couple of hours later with a throat-searing thirst. Water just didn't cut it. I'd been overcome with bloodlust, although I didn't know that's what it was at the time.

Yep. I'd nearly murdered my fiancé. The night he'd proposed.

After taking care of him with the healing qualities of her own blood, Sindi whisked me away from civilization before I could kill anyone and taught me how to control the thirst. It took a while—and a lot of fights with Sindi and many nights locked up in her storage room to keep me from becoming a murderer—but I eventually grew to the point where animal blood sustained my body and actual human food satisfied my hunger. Once I knew I'd be okay, I thought I'd give the Ryan and Kaela Show another chance. But I was too late. He'd already moved on, of course. He'd moved right on top of my best friend. I couldn't blame either of them, though. After all, they didn't even know I existed. How could they know the betrayal I felt?

Once inside the townhouse Sindi and I shared—well, she shared with me since it was hers long before she met me—I found my laptop open on the coffee table in the living room. A swipe of the trackpad proved the truth of her story: on the screen was an open email. Weird. I hadn't seen it this morning. I dropped down onto the couch to read.

Dear Ms. Peters,

After reviewing your history and qualifications, we believe you are a perfect fit for the Night Manager position at Whisper Falls Inn in the beautiful mountains of Colorado, and we're excited to offer you the job. We have outlined the terms of employment, including compensation, below. If you agree with our conclusion, we would like you to start as soon as possible. We understand you may need time to consider our offer, but we hope you will respond quickly so we may start making preparations for your arrival.

Yours truly,

M. Luiza

The rest of the email outlined a modest salary enhanced by free lodging and meals but failed to provide any other details, such as an address or even city.

"Spam is getting weirder by the day," I muttered as I closed the email, cursing spammers and hackers. I wondered what this joker's end-game was. What did they get out of a fake job offer?

Not two seconds later, another message popped up, opening itself.

Ms. Peters,

We apologize that in our excitement of offering you the job, we failed to provide necessary details. Our inn is located in what we like to think of as the prettiest and most charming small town in the world. We are surrounded by majestic mountains and forestland with a larger variety of wildlife than anywhere else in the state, perhaps the country. While the area offers much to do, from skiing to hunting to art classes, we have safeguards in place that ensure our hometown remains a lovely place to live, not just to visit. We've attached a few pictures so you can see for yourself why we believe you will quickly learn to call it home and the people family.

Yours truly (again),

M. Luiza

A slideshow began to play at the bottom of the message, featuring gorgeous photos of a small town nestled in a cradle of purple mountains with snowcapped peaks.

"Awesome," I muttered as my hand moved the cursor to X out of the window. "Virus must already be installed."

My finger lowered over the trackpad and was about to press down when the slideshow displayed a photo that made my breath catch, and not because of its beauty. A large Victorian manor, complete with turrets and gingerbread trim, forced my pause. *How do I know that place?* The sense of familiarity poked angrily at the back of my mind. The photo changed, focused in on the plaque by the manor's front door: Whisper Falls Inn, Est. 1854.

Home.

The word floated through my mind, not as a premonition or wishful thinking as the letter promised, but heavily laced with nostalgia. The townhome's living room in front of me disappeared as other, seemingly random images hijacked my vision. Images of what could have been the rooms inside the inn, followed by portraits and snapshots of people. Faces that I felt deep down I should know. A close-up of a woman with long, dark hair like mine . . . gray-green eyes, the same shade and shape as mine.

Home.

"What the hell?" I slammed my finger down on the pad, closing out the message, and shut the laptop before jumping back in my seat, as though the message could hurt me. My heart raced, and I struggled to breathe. I curled into a ball on the couch and glared at the offensive machine on the coffee table. After several moments, my heart settled and everything returned to normal. Another few moments and I couldn't remember what had caused such a visceral reaction. "I'm losing my damn mind."

Sindi had warned me about vampires losing their sanity, but always in relation to being starved of blood. I was not starved of blood, nor of food. Well, I didn't eat earlier. I unfolded myself from the sofa and headed for the kitchen to find something for . . . I glanced at the clock on the stove. 11:48 p.m. Something for brunch.

As I cooked and ate, my mind wandered back to Sindi's orders and the fake job offer. Maybe it wasn't real, but it got me to thinking. Hotel night manager wasn't exactly what I'd had in mind when I switched my major from pre-med to business after I'd turned and then continued with night classes to earn my event planning certification, thinking event planners worked at night. They did, but, turned out, not *only* at night. But maybe there was potential here. After all, hotels hosted events and many at night. I'd taken the bartending job to grow into a special events planner at the club, but it'd been more than a year and that had gone nowhere. And this was a full-time, salaried position with benefits in a place so far away, it didn't get reception for the Ryan & Heather Super Sappy Love Show.

The small-town part, though . . . I'd come to Atlanta in the first place to escape the small-town life of my childhood. I'd done quite well in putting that misery behind me, never thinking about home and the family that had taken me in only because they had to, but didn't really want me. I'd escaped that life once. Did I really want to go back? Of course, the pictures of the mountain village looked nothing like the dusty Texas town where I'd grown up. Maybe Colorado small towns were different.

"Yeah, right." I dropped my plate in the dishwasher and cleaned up the rest of the kitchen before sitting down to clean up my computer.

After the virus scan came back clean, I went on an online hunt for a new job—hotel night manager. Every single listing I found on every single job site was the same one: Whisper Falls Inn.

CHAPTER 2

"Sleep well?" Sindi asked me the next night when I came into the kitchen, a teasing glint in her eye and smirk on her lips.

I groaned with embarrassment. "Did I . . . make noises?"

She shrugged. "How would I know? I sleep like the dead."

Bada-bing. It was one of her favorite lines, but it grew old two years ago. I rolled my eyes.

"But I can smell it." Her smirk grew.

My cheeks flushed. Sometimes, I wished my vampirism was more like hers. She couldn't blush.

"All sweet and sexy at the same time," she added.

"Ugh. Sindi! Stop."

She placed a glass of blood in front of me—our version of the protein smoothie. "But it's such a delightful way to wake up—horny as hell. Starts the night off right."

"Not when it's the only action you're getting," I muttered.

"Speak for yourself." She swatted me on the ass before heading back upstairs to get ready for work.

I lifted the glass to my mouth and forced the cool liquid down. Stored blood compared to fresh blood like fat-free cheese compared to the real deal —it just flat-out didn't. I should have left the city last night to hunt out in the country, but I'd promised Sindi I'd wait for her to make the trip on our next shared night off. *Whenever that might be.* It'd been weeks since we'd hunted, and the blood we'd collected then was running low. The thought of living in a small town surrounded by forest and wildlife admittedly sounded more and more appealing. *I could drink fresh every night . . .*

If only I could find a job in a place that actually existed. I was letting the fictional Whisper Falls Inn get to me—and it had to be fictional, because all the weirdness last night just couldn't be real. *That reminds me. I need to take my computer in to Joe tonight.*

After finishing my blood, I downed a cup of coffee before jumping into the shower. Visions from my dream floated lazily behind my closed lids as I stood under the flowing water—full lips traveling over my neck and shoulder . . . large hands skimming down my side . . . my tongue playing over the birthmark on his muscular chest . . . gray-green eyes, darker than my own, piercing all the way into me, touching my soul . . .

I'd never admitted that last part to Sindi, not really even to myself. Because those eyes—I felt like I knew them, except I didn't. The rest was all Ryan, I was sure of it. I'd been dreaming of him since the day I met him freshman year at Emory University. But for some reason, all my dreams had those eyes that looked nothing like Ryan's warm brown ones. The intense feeling that came with those eyes, what they did to my heart and soul, could only mean they'd belonged to my ex back in Texas. The one whose memory I'd chosen to bury, but my subconscious thought we should bring out on a regular basis, like whenever I was horny.

"I need to get laid," I muttered as I towel-dried my hair.

"Yes, you do!" Sindi called from her own bathroom. She didn't have to yell. I could hear her as well as she could hear me. As though realizing this, she dropped her voice to normal tones. "I bet Colorado lumberjacks are great in bed. What else do they have to do with their free time?"

"I'm pretty sure not everyone in Colorado is a lumberjack."

"Maybe not, but they sure are sexy. You're gonna get so lucky."

"I'm not even going. Just stop it already."

"Yes, you are."

"It wasn't real."

"If you say so. Or maybe it's very real and they really want you and you just can't admit that to yourself."

"How would they even know what skills or experience I have?" Or didn't have, as it was.

She appeared in my doorway, her head tilted as she secured her earing while watching me with a raised brow. "Are you telling me not once after graduation or since did you put your résumé on the internet? And if you say no, I'll have to kick your ass." She barely paused, not letting me answer, because she already knew I had. "So someone obviously, *finally* found it, and they want you. Don't look a gift horse in the mouth, Kaela. Take the damn job."

"If I didn't know any better, I'd say you're trying to get rid of me," I said between breaths as I did the necessary dance to tug on my tight black jeans. "Something you want to tell me?"

When she didn't answer immediately, I glanced up to find something dark flicker across her blue eyes, but they cleared instantly. "Yeah. Start your career. Get your own place. And then *I'm* coming to stay with *you* this time. Maybe I can meet a sexy lumberjack who doesn't mind sharing his bed and his blood every night."

She threw me a wink before spinning and sauntering back to her room.

~

"I HAVE to make a stop on the way to work, okay?" I said a half-hour later as we left home, indicating my laptop bag on my shoulder. "I just need to drop it off with Joe. It'll be quick, I promise."

Sindi lifted a perfectly shaped brow. "We can't be late again."

"We won't. I swear." I held up my pinky as we began walking down the residential street toward Peachtree Road and the nightclub we both bartended at tonight. We didn't actually do the whole pinky-swear thing—the finger lift was enough in our book.

"I'm pretty sure we're both out of warnings," she reminded me.

"We'll be fine. It'll only take a second. And if you want to go on, you can."

"Yeah, sure, because if *you* get fired, you already have another job waiting for you."

I ignored the comment. She refused to believe the job offer was a fake, and I couldn't prove it until my computer was professionally scanned and remedied. So it was a moot point to argue any further about it.

Joe's computer repair shop was right around the corner from home and a few blocks from the club, on the second floor over one of the many restaurants and bars lining the street. I'd insisted Sindi go on without me because we both knew she was a lot closer to losing her job than I was. So I couldn't believe it when I came out of Joe's and saw her crimson head bobbing in a small crowd in front of one of the restaurants. I pushed by a few people and tapped on her shoulder.

"What the hell are you doing?" I demanded, unable to see what she could considering she stood taller than most of the crowd, while I stared at people's backs. "I thought you didn't want to get fired."

She glanced down at me before looking forward again. Then as though something spooked her, she looked at me again with wide eyes. She grabbed my upper arm and started tugging me back out of the crowd.

"Hey!" I said. "What's going on?"

"Nothing. Come on. We have to go, right?"

The crowd gasped as we began to make our way around it without stepping into the busy street.

"There's the ring," someone squealed excitedly.

I looked over with curiosity. Did I mention how much I enjoyed sappy love stories? That's when I noticed exactly which restaurant everyone had gathered in front of. I shouldn't have been surprised. The Bird Cage, a fancy, romantic gig famous for the number of proposals that took place on the little metal gazebo out front. The place where Ryan had proposed to me. I usually avoided it, crossing the road to walk on the other side ever since. I hadn't been paying attention when I'd come out of Joe's.

"You think she'll say yes?" someone asked.

"So romantic!" another sighed.

I stopped, unable to help myself. I was drawn in along with everyone else. I peeked through a small gap in the crowd to see what looked like men's legs bent down on one knee.

"Kaekae, come on!" Sindi insisted.

"You go on if you want. I just want to see."

"No. You don't."

I shook my arm free from her grip and threw her a harsh look. "I'm fine. It's not like I can avoid this place or public proposals the rest of my life. In fact, they make me happy."

"You do *not* want to see this one. It won't make you happy. Trust me."

"Why n—" As I looked in her eyes, realization dawned on me.

Go. Just move along, get to work, and go on with your night. I tried to convince myself, but did I mention what a masochist I was? My feet carried me closer, and I pressed into the crowd, ignoring the jabs and comments about my rudeness. I was a woman possessed, by what I didn't know, but I couldn't stop myself until I was at the front of the crowd. And I couldn't stop the sob when I saw them.

Ryan on one knee, just like he'd been that terrible night.

Ryan holding a small, black box up, just like he'd been that terrible night.

Ryan smiling with that nervous tic where his dark hair touched his temple, just like he'd been that terrible night.

And Heather, her curly hair bouncing as she jumped up and down in her slinky dress and heels, which she'd also been doing that terrible night.

But she hadn't been the one squealing, "YES!"

She'd been out here, right where I stood, excited for me.

I'd been the one saying, "Yes!"

I couldn't say what overcame me. Every possible emotion known to man, or vampire, whatever. At least, all of the negative ones, exploding with the intensified force of my kind. Tears burned my eyes. Sobs choked me, making me gasp for air. Hurt, denial, sadness, anger—they all swirled together inside me.

People started screaming. And running. And I didn't know why.

Heather cried out. Ryan ducked and tried to push her behind him. She grabbed onto him as she tripped, ripping his dress shirt open as they both went down, him on top of her. He held his arms up, as though trying to stop something from hitting them.

"Kaela." Sindi's voice came from a great distance, muffled by the whir of blood rushing through my ears.

I couldn't turn to look at her. My vision tunneled onto the scene in front of me, through a thick, red haze. Heather splayed out on the ground, Ryan on top of her, his shirt hanging open, baring his chest. The gazebo, shaped like a bird cage, appeared to be collapsing over them. Several support bars snapped free, and the ends twisted inward, all pointing at Ryan, closing in on him.

"Kaela!" Sindi's voice came more urgently now. A vice grabbed my upper arm and jerked at me. "Kaela, stop this! Now!"

She tugged me again, harder now, twisting me away. I looked at her and blinked with disorientation.

"Stop," she said much more calmly, her blue eyes locked on mine. I tried to look back, but she moved her face, blocking my line of sight. "No more, Kaekae. No more."

I blinked again. My head cleared. My lungs seized. "Oh my god! What did I do?"

She tried to stop me from looking again, but I had to know. I shifted to see around her and threw my hand over my mouth. Heather and Ryan were crawling out of a gap in the metal bars of the gazebo, which looked like a large hand had squeezed the top of it like a beer can. Except, some of the bars appeared to be partially melted. *Metal* bars. *Melted.*

"Come on. We need to get out of here." Sindi took my hand and tugged me along behind her. I stumbled in my heeled boots at first, but caught myself and followed without paying attention to where we went. We walked in silence for a while, how long I didn't know, as I was lost in my own mind. We finally stopped, and Sindi turned to me. "Are you going to make it through your shift?"

I realized we stood at the back door of the club, a metal door in a brick building. My hand lifted to the door, but nothing happened. It didn't melt or crumple under my touch. I inhaled a deep breath and nodded. "I'm okay. I'll be okay."

She studied my face for a moment and nodded, although she didn't look entirely convinced. She shouldn't have been. I was far from okay. I was a mess at work, making the wrong drinks, dropping glasses, giving incorrect change. My mind was still stuck on the proposal. On the deformed bird cage gazebo. On Ryan's bare chest.

That didn't have a birthmark.

For some reason, that's what my mind obsessed on the most. If he didn't have a birthmark, then he wasn't the one in my dreams. And if he wasn't, who the hell was?

"You need to take that job and get far away from here," Sindi said once we were home.

I sat on the couch in a ball with my legs drawn in and a blanket wrapped around me. I stared at her blankly.

"You could have killed him, Kaela. Again."

My eyes squeezed shut, and I nodded. "I know," I whispered.

"It must happen when you lose control of your emotions," she said, referring to the deformed metal. "Or when you're angry or hurt or something."

I nodded again. Something similar had happened before. Only once, the first time I'd seen Ryan and Heather together, through the window of the apartment he and I used to share, both naked in our bed. The entire metal fire escape bent and melted before I turned away and ran. Sindi had followed me there, just in case things went bad with Ryan and me as I was making the first move to try to start over with him. She'd witnessed the whole thing.

"And as long as you're here and they're here . . . well, it's not good for you. And it sure as hell isn't good for them."

She was right. I couldn't deny it anymore. I had to shed my masochistic tendencies and do what I should have done a long time ago. Otherwise, I'd never be able to move on. And if I killed one of them, I'd never be able to live with myself.

"What about you?" I asked her, my voice thin.

She gave me a warm smile and patted my knee. "I keep telling you. I'm a big girl. I'll be fine. You helped me through a rough time, too, gave me a distraction from my own shitty life. But I'm good now." Her smile broadened. "You and me, we had a lot of fun together. We got through some fucked-up shit, but we had a lot of fun, too, right?"

I smiled weakly and nodded.

"So we're good. And now it's time for you to spread your wings and fly, baby bird." She leaned over and gave me a quick hug. Something she didn't do very often. She was much more of a badass vampire chick than I was. "Besides, I'm not kidding. Once you're settled, my ass is so out there to visit. It'll be a long drive, so you better make it worth it."

She handed me my phone and a piece of paper with the number for Whisper Falls Inn. Why was I not surprised she'd written it down from the email? She stared at me expectantly. She'd never give up until I proved to her the inn was a hoax. So I dialed the number and tapped the green send icon.

"Whisper Falls Inn," the sweet female voice on the other end answered, surprising me.

Sindi laughed at my shocked expression, then nodded with encouragement.

"Um . . . hi. This is Kaela Peters. I'm calling for M. Luiza. About a job offer."

CHAPTER 3

*A*fter spending the day in a nearby motel waiting for night to fall, I pulled into the McDonald's parking lot in Durango, Colorado, exactly two weeks later. As Ms. Luiza had promised, I couldn't have missed the shuttle bus parked in back that I was supposed to meet. A huge wrap around the entire vehicle advertised the beauty and fun to be had in Havenwood Falls, my soon-to-be hometown. Several people were boarding the bus. I parked my car nearby and glanced at the clock. 7:14. I had just enough time to pee and grab something to eat before we hit the road again.

"Holy fuck, it's freezing!" I yelped when I opened my car door. I grabbed the thick, white coat from the passenger seat and wrapped myself up before climbing out.

"Michaela Petran?" a deep and raspy voice said from behind me, and I turned to face an old man with gray, shaggy hair and a long beard to match, wearing a thick flannel shirt, jeans, and boots. I had to bite back a smirk, thinking of Sindi's lumberjack dreams.

"Um . . . Kaela Peters," I corrected as I pulled on my coat. How was he not freezing?

His gray, furry brows pinched together before laughter twinkled in his blue eyes. "Of course! Silly me! Gettin' forgetful in my old age. Anyway, good on you for meetin' us here. The drive from here on in can get confusin' and treacherous. You sure you want to drive it?"

"I'm sure. I'll be fine," I promised. It wasn't like I really had a choice. I needed my car.

He eyed said car. "In that thing?" He chuckled. "Good thing the roads are clear right now. But winter ain't over yet up in the mountains. You better be gettin' a four-wheel-drive A-S-A-P."

"Um . . . thanks for the advice," I said. I supposed most of my savings would be going to a new vehicle soon. "I'll be fine for now, right?"

"For now," he said with a nod. "Alrighty then, Ms. Petra—I mean, Ms. Peters. I'm waitin' on a few more arrivals, but we leave in ten minutes with or without them and with or without you."

"Understood." I gave him a smile, then hurried inside to take care of my personal business, worried about being left behind.

For some odd reason, I couldn't find Havenwood Falls anywhere on any map, not even Google's. I had coordinates, but Ms. Luiza warned me that GPS often led people down the wrong roads, taking them hours out of their way. After being on the road for three nights, I really didn't want to add hours if I didn't have to, especially if it risked me being outside at sunrise. So I made sure to be back in my car and ready to go by the time the bus, decorated with ski slopes and restaurant facades, pulled out. To my surprise, I wasn't the only car following. A five-vehicle caravan made its way up and around the mountains.

The roads were steep, twisty, and pitch black except where the beams of our headlights bounced off rock walls on one side and plunging cliffs on the other, with plenty of thick-trunked trees that would split a car in two with one wrong turn. My old Ford Fiesta fell behind at one point, and I rounded a bend and almost slammed into a herd of elk starting to cross the road. I swore they stood at least three feet taller than my car because all I saw at first were legs.

Once I saw the sign welcoming me to Havenwood Falls, I could finally loosen my white-knuckled grip on the steering wheel, damned glad I was part of the caravan, because Ms. Luiza and the old man were right—I'd have never found this place on my own, especially in the dark.

A spotlight lit up the welcome sign, made of layered stone with beautifully made black metal lettering. At once, it was both charming and sinister, as I imagined living in a small mountain town surrounded by the wild would be. My stomach began to flutter with butterflies as the giddiness of my new adventure overcame me for the hundredth time in the last two weeks. Yet, at the same time, a feeling of comfort slid over my shoulders and down my back, like a warm blanket, a comforting hug, a lovingly whispered *welcome home.*

We drove on several miles past the welcome sign, curved another bend, climbed a little higher, and even before I saw them, I knew there'd be lights as soon as we crested the ridge ahead. And there were. A smattering of lights lit up the town below with silhouettes of the looming mountains inky black against the night sky, their white caps appearing to glow. Even in the dark, I felt their intimidating yet wondrous presence. Realization that I'd never see them in the daylight hit me like a punch in the gut. Maybe once I hung my blackout curtains and took certain precautions, I could take a quick peek.

We passed Creekwood, a housing development on the left, then the road forked, but I already knew to stay to the right. And not just because Ms. Luiza had given me directions to the inn from here. I could somehow see in my mind's eye each landmark even before I came to it: Havenstone, a townhouse and villa development built in a wooden ski-lodge style, on the right; the high school's large brick building on the left; a shopping center and an apartment complex (Havenwood Village, I somehow knew) on the right; and then I'd reach the town square. Staying on the same road along the south side of the square, I passed by a two-story row of darkened shops and what I assumed to be apartments above them, considering the lights glowing in a couple windows. Then finally I came to the large Victorian manor that was the inn, sitting at an angle on the corner so it faced the square, a dim light glowing through the glass door. But the inn wasn't exactly as the pictures had promised and what I'd envisioned. Even in the dark, it looked as though it had seen better days—more than a few years ago.

A little old woman wearing an old-fashioned dressing gown stood in the driveway flapping her arms, waving me down although I was already turning toward her. She motioned me along as she scrambled as fast as her little legs could carry her down the drive toward the back of the inn. She could move surprisingly fast considering her age and plump stature. She waved me into a parking space next to the last of five cottages lining the back of the property. Exactly like I'd seen in my mind a few weeks ago.

The woman clapped her hands together under her chin, and a big smile filled her sweet face when I climbed out of the car, making her gray eyes twinkle. "Oh, honey, I'm so glad you're here!"

Her arms opened, and she took a step toward me as though she wanted to hug me, but stopped herself. "I'm sorry! It's just so exciting to have you finally back. I mean, finally here. Back here, in your cottage, yes, that's what I mean. This is your place, dear." She bustled up the steps of the front porch, stood by the front door, and gestured at it. "I'll let you do the honors."

She moved to the side and waited for me to ascend the porch and enter.

"You must be Ms. Luiza," I said as I mounted the steps and held my gloved hand out to her. Damn was I thankful I let Sindi talk me into buying a bunch of winter clothes before I left, all on end-of-the-season sale in Atlanta.

"Madame Luiza, dear. The M has always been for Madame. I'm too old to be a Ms." She patted her gray mop of hair and again motioned at the knob while completely ignoring my outstretched hand. "You should have everything you need for now, and I'll help you get situated for good over the next few days before your first day at work."

I gave her a wary smile before opening the door and crossing the threshold into a small living room that couldn't have been more perfectly decorated for me if I'd done it myself. The cozy room's walls were painted a light neutral color with white trim and was furnished with a plump-cushioned taupe couch and a dark brown chaise lounge set between a large bookcase and a fireplace. Blankets and quilts draped over the sofa and chaise, and flames licked the logs inside the hearth.

"Thought you might like a warm fire to greet you. It's a bit colder here than Georgia, I imagine," Madame Luiza said from behind me.

I snickered. "Just a bit. I'm surprised I can't see my breath."

"Well, that's silly. It's forty-one degrees out. That's a heat wave for this time of year." She emphasized her statement by fanning her face with her hand and letting out a chortle. "That's supposed to change by the end of the week, and we'll be back to cold for a bit longer. But don't you worry. You'll get used to it one of these days." She babbled on as I moved farther into the cottage, glancing around at what I could see through the doorways—a kitchen and a small hallway that led to a bedroom and bathroom. "In a year or two from now, you'll be hitting the swimming hole in June with the rest of the young'uns. I'd go, but ain't nobody want to see this old lady in a bathing suit!"

She chortled again, the sound warming my heart. Rather than annoying me, as it normally would have done, her babbling came as a comfort.

"Well, I'll let you get on then. Sun'll be up in no time, which means our guests will be, too. You get some rest, and I'll see you soon enough."

I stood in the doorway to the kitchen and turned toward her. "It probably won't be until later tomorrow, probably in the evening. I've been driving for days and . . ."

She waved her hand in dismissal. "Oh, I know, honey. No worries. We'll get that all taken care of tomorrow night. Get your tattoo and everything. Or I could probably get Adelaide to come here, make it easier—"

I cut her off. "Um . . . *tattoo?*"

Her eyes widened as she clapped her hands over her mouth. "Did I say that out loud? I'm sorry. I'm trying so hard not to throw everything on you at once. Go on now. There are refreshments in the refrigerator. Bedroom is that way, and blackout curtains throughout. Sleep well!"

She gestured toward the back of the cottage, then hurried out the front door before I could say another word. I followed her, but she was already completely out of sight when I stepped onto the porch.

"What in the hell?" I muttered out loud as I went back out to my car to grab the necessities. I'd unpack the rest tomorrow night.

After dropping my suitcase in my room and kicking my shoes off to replace them with socks and slippers, I padded into the kitchen for something to drink. And nearly squealed when I opened the refrigerator door and saw the bottle on the top shelf.

"Yes! Wine!" The next best thing to blood, but without knowing my way around yet and with sunrise less than two hours away, I wasn't about to go out and hunt tonight. I found a set of wine glasses in the cabinet and a bottle opener in the drawer. This place really was stocked perfectly for me. And when I opened the bottle and took a whiff, I realized just how perfectly.

Too perfectly.

My hands began to shake.

"Blood."

How the hell did they know?

I paced the lovely cottage for hours, unable to settle down and sleep even when the sun rose, which was only barely noticeable behind the total black-out curtains on every window, keeping the interior dark and comfortable. My gut instinct swung erratically between being completely freaked out that my new employers were apparently aware of my state of unusual existence and feeling completely comforted and welcomed by their considerate gestures. I obviously knew other vampires existed in this world because, well, Sindi, and the small handful of others she'd introduced me to. And not to mention whoever had turned me—we'd never figured that out.

Whoever they were was a total dick, leaving me to turn and adapt all on my own. It could have been a bloody disaster with a high body count if not for Sindi. We'd heard rumors of other types of supernatural beings as well, although nobody we knew had ever actually met any others. But what were the chances that the owners of Whisper Falls Inn not only understood that vampires existed, but knew that I was one?

Probably the same chances that every hotel night manager job on the internet was at the same place. And the same chances that you'd seen in your mind the very grounds you drove up to tonight, the very cottage you're in now. The same chances that you feel like you've been here before when you've never even stepped foot in the state of Colorado.

So maybe the owners were also vampires, and they'd heard of me through the vampy grapevine. That was plausible, I supposed. But the rest didn't add up. This place wasn't right. Or maybe I wasn't. Maybe I had gone insane after all.

I stood at the front window, next to the front door, aching to go outside and prove to myself that I did not know that there was a coffee shop three doors down to the west and another on the far side of the square, right across from the chamber of commerce. That there was no way I knew that four blocks to the east of town square and two blocks north, at the end of a cul-de-sac, sat a large log cabin with a green tin roof and a stream running along the back of the property. These kinds of details weren't on the Havenwood Falls website I'd skimmed through after taking the job. So there was no way I knew these things. I had to be wrong.

My legs carried me across the living room, into the kitchen, and back again, trying to expel the nervous energy that had been coursing through my veins since I discovered bottled blood in my fridge. I cursed my vampirism for holding me hostage in here—but, in truth, my avoidance of severe pain was my true captor. I wouldn't die if I went outside. At least, not immediately. But it would sure hurt like hell and leave me all blistery and fucked-up for days. However, I *could* look out the window, at least for a few moments, with no painful repercussions.

I hurried to the bedroom and fished in my suitcase for the sunglasses I held onto for those times when I just needed a peek to remember what the world was like in the light of day. I'd almost trashed the shaded specs while packing, because I'd learned long ago to stop indulging in those little glimpses. They only depressed me. It was better to try to forget life as a normal person and embrace my new existence as a creature of the night. Now I was glad I'd thrown them into the suitcase at the last minute.

After pulling on a hoodie and gloves to cover as much skin as possible, I put on the shades and pushed the front curtain back a few inches. My heart pulsed with longing at the bright world out there . . . except I couldn't really see much. The roof over the front porch blocked out almost everything. I could see my car and the white trunks of aspen trees on the other side of it, an expanse of brown lawn that stretched out from the cottages to the wrap-around porch of the extremely large Victorian-era main building of the inn, and a portion of said porch with its peeling paint that might have been white at one time. Flower beds surrounded the porch, but only a few scraggly vines stuck out of them. I tilted my head and adjusted my angle to catch a glimpse of a brick building across the street, but that was about it.

Fuck.

I was about to let go of the curtain when a blue, late model pickup truck parked about halfway up the drive that led back to the cottages. A moment later, a man walked across the lawn toward the main house, a tool belt hanging low on his hips over his perfectly fitting jeans cladding his perfectly sculpted ass. My breath became lodged in my throat as I drank him in. Tall, broad-shouldered, arms thick with muscles that strained the sleeves of his green Henley. He wore a knit cap, sunglasses, and a closely trimmed beard, preventing me from seeing his face. With my eyes, anyway. Because in my mind, I could see him clearly. He glanced over his shoulder, directly toward me, and I let the curtain fall. Not that he could have possibly seen me from that distance and behind the window under the shadow of the roof . . . but it was a compulsive reaction.

The lump in my throat grew, making it difficult to breathe. *I . . . know . . . him. In all the ways a woman could know a man.*

CHAPTER 4

*T*shook my head and then the rest of my body, shaking off the impossible feeling. The exhaustion of the move, the drive, and everything else finally slammed into me. My body must have pumped through the last of the adrenaline from discovering the blood bottle and now I was crashing. *I just need sleep. This will all make sense after I've had some rest.*

After a quick shower to wash off the travel stink, my head hit the pillow, and I was out.

Full lips skate over my jaw and up to the corner of my mouth. His tongue flicks out, over my bottom lip, before he sucks it in between his. I moan and press my body against his, digging my fingers into the skin of his shoulders as his mouth assaults mine. His hand splays on my lower back, pulling me in tighter against his thigh that's between my legs. I whimper from the friction as my breasts swell and tighten against his bare chest. Needing a breath, I pull away for a moment. My finger traces the birthmark over his heart as my gaze slowly slides upward to meet his. Beautiful gray eyes flecked with green stare back at me.

"You shouldn't be here," he says, although his voice calls me home.

I awoke with a start, my heart pounding a hard rhythm against my ribs. My eyes swept around the unfamiliar room as my mind tried to remember where I was. Oh, right. Freakwood Falls. *Home.* I drifted back to sleep almost immediately.

A light knock on the door brought me out of a deep, dreamless slumber, and I was relieved to see night had fallen. *Now I can get answers.* I threw on a robe before hurrying for the door as another knock sounded. When I pulled it open, Madame Luiza was about to descend the stairs off the porch.

She turned around, and a bright smile lit up her face. "Oh, you *are* up! I was beginning to think I came too early. You're probably exhausted from all that driving. I can come back later, if you'd like, and we can get you all set up with the important stuff then."

She made to turn again, but I stopped her. "No! Wait! I need answers. Now."

A frown momentarily marred her sweet features. "Oh, dear, you are all worked up, aren't you? I should have known. Tsk tsk. I'm so sorry. Here you were, stuck here all day, too. But we'll get that taken care of in a jiffy. The Court is expecting you."

I blinked as my still sleep-fogged mind tried to catch up. "The court? Why?"

Was it really necessary to change my driver's license and car registration my first night here? And how would the court even be open now?

"Well, you have to sign into the Registry and get your mark." She said this as though I should have known what she spoke about.

I lifted a brow. "My mark? As in the tattoo you mentioned last night?"

Realization dawned on her wrinkled face. "Oh, there I go again, getting ahead of myself. You have no idea what I'm talking about, do you?"

I shook my head.

"No worries. Adelaide will explain everything and take good care of you. As long as you follow the rules and laws, you'll be fine."

"This Adelaide will explain everything?" I asked, and she nodded. "Then take me to her. Now."

Madame Luiza gave me a once-over. "Don't you want to put on something a little . . . um . . . *warmer?*"

I glanced down at my nearly naked body clothed in only a short, terrycloth robe barely covering the important parts. I'd been too concerned about answers to even notice the cold. "Oh my god. Of course."

I turned to rush inside and change, but Madame Luiza stopped me. "As soon as you're dressed, you can head on over to the Court. It's across the town square, at the back of City Hall. You can't miss it. There's an emblem with a sun and a moon over the door."

"You're not taking me?"

She smiled warmly. "Oh, no, honey. I have guests to take care of. Doing your job—and everyone else's—for now."

"Do you need help?"

"Yes, but that's what you're here for, right? I can manage another day or two while you get settled. It's important you take care of everything with the Court first. Don't want to get in their bad graces already."

Thirty minutes later, I hurried down my porch steps, bundled in my new coat, hat, and gloves, and focused on finding this court, whatever it was, but more importantly, this Adelaide, who could give me answers. When I set foot on the inn's lawn, though, I had to stop for a moment and close my eyes to take it all in. I inhaled the cold air deeply—or tried to. My lungs struggled to pull as hard as I wanted to, and it took me a moment to remember the thinner air at this altitude. I'd been warned about that.

Still, I sucked in enough to savor the clean, crisp fragrance in my nose and taste on my tongue. Freezing cold, but all natural, the earthiness of aspen, pine, and dirt. Several different food aromas lingered from neighbors' dinners, combining with the smoky warmth of burning wood. Barely a hint of gas fumes, oil, asphalt, or even concrete.

I listened to small animals scurrying into their nests for the night along with the muted chatter of people in their homes and the low hum of television shows. From somewhere not too far away came the sound of people in a bar and nearby there, patrons in restaurants and coffee shops. The sound of tires on roads was definitely present, but not like the nonstop whooshing of the big city. There was still a cacophony of sound here for my vampire ears, but one that was actually calming rather than irritating.

A light breeze kissed my face, chilling my skin, and I was brought out of the moment. My eyes opened, but I hesitated, and for the first time since arriving, I really looked around. The three story inn with its turrets, many bay windows, and gingerbread trim stood ahead at an angle to the corner, its back to me. To my left and slightly behind me was the row of cottages that provided five of the eighteen guest rooms—well, minus one for me now—and beyond them, near the street going north and south, was a small and noticeably empty parking lot. To my right was the driveway that led to the cottages, each one with its own space behind me. All but mine was also empty. Were all the guests Madame Luiza had to tend to still at dinner? And nobody stayed at the inn to eat? I thought I remembered it having its own dining room, supposedly with rave reviews.

The thoughts about the state of the inn drifted away as my gaze lifted to the mountains beyond the structure, soaring thousands of feet high. In awe, I turned in a slow, complete circle, and they were everywhere, boxing this little town in. I guessed that's why they called it a box canyon. Up to the tree line, the mountainsides were dark with forest, and the jagged edges of their white peaks seemed to scrape the stars in the sky. And those stars . . .

"Holy. Shit," I whispered. I'd always half-believed pictures of the night sky with this many stars—and so close!—were fakes. I gasped as I turned in a circle again, now while staring at the sky. "That's the fucking Milky Way!"

I lifted my arms and waved my fingers in the air as though I could actually touch it.

"It's so magical." The words came out softly, barely audible to my own sensitive ears, but they were followed by what sounded like a snort from the direction of the inn's wraparound porch.

I dropped my head, and my gaze swept across the porch, but I saw nobody there. Chills rose anew over my skin, and I tightened my coat around me as I began to walk again when a scream and a crash came from inside the main house. I immediately bolted to it, across the lawn and at the door in less than a second before remembering myself. Not that any witnesses were around, considering all the empty parking spaces.

"Madame Luiza?" I called as I rushed through one set of French doors and into a parlor room. I heard a whimper and a faint heartbeat a level above me. I hurried through the parlor, past the empty and dark dining room, and into the lobby before turning for the curving staircase, taking two steps at a time. Not until I stopped at the end of the hallway, where Madame Luiza lay, did I realize I'd known exactly where to find her and how to get here.

"I'm . . . okay." The old woman's gasp came from the floor, and I dropped to my knees by her side. What appeared to have been a tea set lay in pieces on the floor, the tea mixing with blood gushing out of a gash in her forearm.

"Oh, no. Here." I peeled off my coat and gloves and lifted my wrist to my mouth to pierce my skin and give her my healing blood, but she gave a minute shake of her head.

"No, no. That . . . won't work," she gasped out. "Just . . . get me . . . to bed." Her voice faded, and her eyelids drooped before closing completely.

I grabbed the tea towel and pressed it to her wound before picking up the little old lady and carrying her into the room that I instinctively knew was hers.

"What happened?" I asked as I lay her down.

Her eyes fluttered open for a moment. "Old . . . lady. Accident."

She fell silent again as her eyes closed.

"What the hell happened? What did you do to her?" The girl's voice demanded in that accusatory tone teenagers always seemed to speak in. She pushed past me and dropped to the old woman's bed, glancing at me long enough to show her disgust before giving Madame Luiza all of her attention.

"What's going on?" a deep voice asked from the doorway, making the hairs on the back of my neck raise. "Oh, fuck. Is she okay?"

The large body pushed past me as well, nearly knocking me over. He knelt down next to the girl, his broad shoulders blocking me from seeing anything else. I took several steps backward before turning to leave the room. I assumed they were her family and would take care of her, so I stood in the dark hallway, not knowing what to do besides wait. Oh, and clean up the mess. Just as I bent down to start picking up the ceramic pieces, the man's body filled the doorway again before he strode right on by me, again without a glance.

"I have to find Isabella," he growled over his shoulder.

"Wait! Don't leave me with her!" the girl shouted, her voice filled with annoyance.

"She's your family, Aurelia. Get over yourself." He disappeared down the stairs then, although I could hear him stomping around the lower level as though looking for something. A moment later, I heard a door open and close.

"Asshole," the girl huffed as she stomped out of the room, also right past me. "I notice *you're* not staying."

She kept talking, although he was long gone. A moment later, she too left through the same door.

I stood there stupidly for a long moment, until Madame Luiza's faint voice called out to me.

"What do you need? What can I do?" I asked as I rushed inside and knelt by her bed.

"Arm," she croaked. I looked down to find the towel, now stained crimson, still pressed against her wound.

"Oh, god, of course! Are you . . . sure?" I held my wrist out.

She gave me a weak smile. "I'm sure, dear. I'm far beyond healing. A bandage will do. Keep me from messing up the bedding any more than I already have."

"Anything else?" I asked. "Water?"

"That would be good."

I hurried back down the stairs and to the kitchen. The first aid kit was exactly where I knew it would be and so were the glasses. I tried not to think about that too much, forcing myself to focus on Madame Luiza. She drifted off while I bandaged her arm, and I couldn't help but notice the odd odor—her blood was not of a healthy human. I tried not to think about that too much either.

When I finished, I lifted her unconscious body into the chaise lounge, the only other piece of furniture in the room besides the bed and a dresser between them. I easily found the closet of linens and changed her bedding, then I studied her, wondering if I should change her, too, or if that would be crossing the line. After all, she was my boss. Undressing her might be going too far.

As I looked more closely at her, I noticed in more detail the lines and curves of her face. I hadn't noticed so many wrinkles last night. I'd thought her hair was a steel-gray then, but now it seemed lighter, with more white strands than I'd realized. She was even older than I'd first thought. And she was running this place by herself? No wonder she'd been so desperate to hire someone! I wondered if she knew how to spam the internet by herself, or if her grandchildren had helped.

Speaking of whom, what the hell happened to them? Did they really just take off and leave her here with a near stranger? I thought they'd gone to get help, but more than an hour had already passed, and still nobody had come.

"Help me?" The little old lady's soft voice jerked my attention from the doorway and back to her. "I'd like to change. Purple dress in the closet."

My eyes squinted as I looked at her. "I don't think you should go out. You need to rest."

She let out a long, sad sigh. "Yes, I know, dear."

"Then wouldn't you be more comfortable in a nightgown?"

She reached up and patted my hand as she gave me yet another weak smile, this one reaching her eyes with a faint twinkle. "Please, dear. I don't want to die in my night clothes."

I returned her smile as I held her hand in mine. "You're not going to die, Madame Luiza. Not on my watch. It's just a cut. The bleeding's already stopped."

She squeezed my hand weakly. "Oh, no, not from that. Look at me and tell me death's not coming. Maybe not tonight, but soon. It's simply my time. I'm the last hold-out. At least you're here, though, honey. That's all I wanted. Now help me put on my favorite dress, will you?"

I gazed at her for a moment, and she was right. I could practically see her aging in front of me. My heart suddenly felt like it weighed three tons. My emotions confused me. I barely knew this woman, but I couldn't deny the deep sadness filling me. Swallowing down the lump in my throat, I nodded.

After changing her into the purple gown that looked as though it had been in fashion at the turn of the *last* century, I helped her lay back down.

"Who can I call?" I asked.

Her eyes fluttered closed. "Nobody, dear."

"But your family—"

"They won't come if you call, but Aurelia and Gabe might come on their own. You're here, honey. That's enough."

I won't let you die alone. She obviously didn't want that if having me here was enough for her. The poor woman was nearly as bad off as I was in the family department. Although it wasn't something I'd say aloud, regardless of how well she seemed to be accepting her imminent death.

She fell asleep almost immediately, although it was a fitful sleep. Afraid to leave her side and not knowing what else to do, I sat on the bed, then paced, then sat on the chaise for a while, then paced some more. Hours passed. The earlier sounds of town square had fallen fairly silent. Aurelia never returned. Neither did the guy, who I assumed to be Gabe. So much for going to court and finding Adelaide. They'd have to wait until tomorrow night. Sunrise was only a few hours away. At least the curtains appeared to be blackouts, so I could stay if nobody came. I stood at the window after inspecting them, watching the moon as it began to set behind the mountain. The sound of a door downstairs barely registered in my mind.

"Adelaide's here for you." The deep voice once again sent a shiver down my spine.

I turned to meet a very familiar pair of eyes that even in the dim light I knew were gray with green flecks.

CHAPTER 5

$\mathcal{W}$e both stood frozen, staring at each other for seconds that stretched into eons. His face was turned down, causing a lock of his dark hair, combed back from his face, to fall forward by his temple. His narrowed eyes gazed up at me, almost accusingly, through thick, black lashes. His dark brows were pinched together, forming two vertical lines between them and several creases across his forehead. My fingers twitched with the desire to smooth them out, to relieve the pain he was obviously in.

The longer we stared, the more I felt like he was trying to reach into my soul and claim it. Or maybe that he already had. My heart beat erratically, and my mouth and throat went dry. The room suddenly became too small for the both of us. For him. And not just because he was far over six feet tall and built like an Olympian. His very presence filled the room completely . . . started to fill me.

"I'll, uh, let you—" I stammered at the same time as he said, "You need to go . . ."

His angry tone made me flinch, and he sounded like he wanted to say more, but then looked like he couldn't be bothered. Another long, awkward moment passed before I could finally will my feet to move. I shuffled forward, and he stepped to the side, and things became even more awkward as we did some strange dance to move around each other in the small space without daring to touch. As though that would scar us for life. Maybe it would.

Somehow I made it out of that room without even brushing against his arm or, you know, accidentally falling on top of his very nicely formed body.

Finally out of the room, I felt like the temperature dropped ten degrees. I had to pause to take a few breaths and settle my speeding heart. Before heading down the hallway to the stairs, I looked over my shoulder to see the god-like figure bending over and planting a kiss on Madame Luiza's forehead. For a fleeting moment, I felt jealousy for her. *Get a grip, Kae. You know nothing about him.*

Except, something way in the back, dark corners of my mind niggled at me, saying I did.

Once I finally gathered my wits back about me, I went down the stairs to meet the mysterious Adelaide who supposedly could answer all my questions. Because of the way Madame Luiza had spoken of her, and maybe also because of her name, I expected to find an older woman, smartly dressed and full of wisdom. Even if it was a ridiculous time of night, or early morning, for such a woman to be out making house calls. What I found was a young woman about my age, wearing a dark purple sweater, ripped up jeans, and knee-high boots. Her light brown hair was pulled back into a messy bun, she wore a diamond stone in her nose, and black-framed glasses added a studious touch to her otherwise edgy appearance. Several rings decorated her fingers.

"Michaela!" she gasped as a hand flew to her mouth. She let out another squeal, this one muffled. "I mean, Kaela, right?"

I blinked. That was the second time someone in this town had called me Michaela. What was wrong with them?

"Um, yeah, Kaela. You must be Adelaide?"

Her mouth twitched as though she fought a frown. "Addie. Please." Her voice dropped and filled with sorrow. "How is Mammie?"

My head cocked to the side.

"Madame Luiza?" she corrected.

I bit my lip. "Not well. I don't know what happened. I think she collapsed from exhaustion, but she's fading so quickly . . . Gabe is up there with her."

Addie's brows jumped up to her hairline. "Gabe is here? I thought he was at my house. The poor kid. What did he do when he saw you? And what about Aurelia? They've been through so much. It's good that you're here . . . Hey, what happened to Xandru? I thought he went up there to get you."

I tried to follow her questions, but they confused me. "Wait. Gabe's a kid?"

Now it was her turn to cock her head and blink at me. "Uh, yeah, he's twelve. I thought you said—"

I pressed my fingers to my temples. "I'm sorry. I don't know anybody here yet. I thought that was Gabe. He was here earlier with Aurelia, but they both took off, looking for an Isabella . . . I'm so confused."

Addie crossed the room to stand in front of me and placed a hand on my shoulder. "It's okay, Mich—I mean, Kaela. You'll get it soon, I'm sure of it."

"So who's up there with Madame Luiza now?" A blush crept across my skin just at the thought of him.

One side of her face pulled up in a knowing smirk. "Judging by the look on your face, that was definitely Xandru. Alexandru Roca, but we call him Xandru or Xan. I'm surprised you don't . . ."

She trailed off, and I waited for her to continue, but she shook her head before gesturing me into the nearby seating area.

"Never mind. Let's get you all taken care of before the sun rises so you can do what you need to do and not have to worry about those pesky UV rays."

She produced an old leather satchel I hadn't noticed before and set it on the floor next to a large cushioned chair that she motioned for me to sit on. I stood in place as she disappeared through a doorway behind the front desk and returned a moment later pushing an office chair on wheels. She sat on it and proceeded to pull what looked like a tattoo kit out of her bag.

"Come on," she said, once again gesturing at the bigger chair. "Don't tell me you're afraid of needles."

"No, and I'm not against tattoos or anything, but, um . . . are you freaking *serious*? I just got to town, just met you people, and you expect me to sit down and say, 'Okay, sure, ink me up. I don't give a shit what you to do my body. That I have to live with for . . . *forever*. Literally! And let's do it right now, even though your new boss is upstairs dying, and who knows what will happen to this place if she does, so you might not even stay, so here, this will give you something to remember your very short visit with us."

"Nobody remembers Havenwood Falls," she muttered.

"*What?*" That was her response to my rant?

She blew out a sigh. "Calm down, Kaela. It's not what you think. You can tell me whatever design you want, where you want it. Anywhere. I've done it all. If you feel more comfortable in a private room, we can go upstairs."

I let out a humorless laugh and threw up my hands. "Unbelievable! You don't get it. What in the *fuck* makes you think I want a damn tattoo?"

She looked up at me and said flatly, "Because it'll allow you to walk in the daylight."

I froze and stared at her, my mouth partially open. She gazed back at me with a brow lifted and her arms crossed, as though challenging me. In less than a heartbeat, I stood right in front of her and snarled, fangs out.

"If you know what I am, then you know you shouldn't fuck with me."

She stood, her face right in front of mine, and her eyes narrowed as her fingers flicked. I was suddenly on my knees, doubled over in pain as though I'd been stabbed in the gut. Then as quickly as it came, the sensation was gone. I slowly stood up and glared at her.

"Did you do that?" I whispered.

"Yeah, and I'll do a lot worse if you ever threaten me again. We're friends, Kaela. I'm on your side." She sat back down and picked up a bottle of ink. "Now, are we going to do this or not?"

"Not."

She looked up in surprise. "You don't want to be able to walk outside in the sun? See the world again in the light of day? Live a little more normally?"

"More than anything," I admitted. "But not until you explain how."

"How what?"

"How . . . everything. How you know what I am. How you did that to me. How your tattoo can allow me to walk in the sun. Oh, and maybe how I feel like I know weird, random things about this town."

She exhaled a long breath. "Fine, I will. As long as you sit down and give me some kind of idea of what you want your tattoo to look like so I can come up with a design."

When she obviously wouldn't say anything else yet, my head tilted to the side. "It'll really allow me to go outside in the day?"

"Yes, and your skin won't burn up or anything. You'll be just like a human in that regard."

"And you know this because . . ."

"Because we give these things out almost every week."

My eyes widened. "There are that many vampires? Here?"

She shrugged. "Well, not all vampires. Other supernaturals, too. They all get marked when they come to town. Everyone gets a benefit from it, but that's how you sign into the Registry so the Court knows who's in town. If they're only visiting, they get temporary ink."

"What's this Court? Madame Luiza kept talking about it."

"I'll explain, I promise. Just sit down already."

After another moment, I dropped into the lumpy chair. "So why can't I get temporary ink?"

Her eyes narrowed. "I guess you can if that's what you want, but you'll just have to get it redone in a couple of weeks."

I considered this for a moment, then nodded. "Okay, then, that's what I want. Just in case."

"In case of what?"

My turn to shrug. "In case you're lying." I frowned. "Or in case she doesn't make it and I don't have a job."

"Pft. You have a job as long as you want one."

"You don't know that."

"Trust me. I do."

"Yeah, well, I don't trust you."

"You will. Now, can we do this?"

I gnawed on the inside of my cheek for a long moment as I stared out the picture window behind her. It was dark now, but how beautiful would that view be in the morning?

"Fine. Temporary ink only," I said out of bull-headedness. "Give me a sun, since that's what this is all about." I paused. "No, wait. A moon. Because I've come to love it."

"How about both?" She pulled a small pad out of her bag and a pencil and quickly sketched out a beautiful image of half a sun and half a moon with a swirly design around it.

"Wow. You're very talented."

"Thanks. I do a lot with suns and moons, because they're such a big part of our lives, you know? With how they affect so many of us, especially here in Havenwood Falls."

I didn't miss her use of "us." She wasn't human, either. But what was she?

She traced over the image with a purple pen, then tore the page off the pad. "Where do you want it?"

I pulled my sweater off, revealing a tank top underneath, and tapped on the back of my right shoulder. "So I'm doing this. Now tell me more. How does this work?"

She sprayed the paper with what I presumed to be water before pressing it against my skin. "The ink is infused with magic."

"Excuse me?" I twisted to stare at her, my mouth again partially open.

"Be still!" She pulled the paper off, wiped my skin, then tried again. I stayed still so it wouldn't smudge this time. "Yes, I said magic. I'm a witch. That's how I brought you to your knees."

"Whoa," I breathed out. "For real?"

"For real. I'm a Beaumont, one of the founding families of the Luna Coven, the main one here in Havenwood Falls." She started setting up her tools and bottles. The black ink shimmered with silver streaks.

"There's more than one coven?"

"Oh, yes. Not everyone wants to do what we have to do, considering our role with the town and the Court." She pushed her sleeves up, revealing tattoos on both forearms, stretched and wiggled her fingers, and then picked up her tool and dipped it in the shimmery ink. "It can get so political. I hate that part, too, but I can't really leave it."

"Why not?"

"I'm being groomed for the High Council. Some day. In probably a few hundred years."

I snickered, thinking she was joking.

"I'm not quite next in line, thank goddess. There's a couple of generations to get through, and we live extremely long lives."

Wow. My questions paused as I considered that. Were there really others, besides Sindi, whom I could possibly be friends with and not have to worry about them growing old when I didn't? Speaking of Sindi, I couldn't wait to call her! She was going to freak. And then be out here in a heartbeat. I knew she should have just come with me. Although, she'd be all over Xandru, and I couldn't let that happen. Maybe I wouldn't tell her right away. At least give myself a chance to be humiliated with rejection before she came out and dug her claws in. Of course, he seemed to be more her type anyway—kind of an asshole.

"So," I continued as the needle worked the ink into my skin, "you're a witch. And there are other supernaturals in this town? Such as . . . ?"

"Mmm . . . such as pretty much all kinds of species and sub-species. Shifters, vampires, mages, fae, sirens, gargoyles, various kinds of magically touched . . . Even hunters."

"And they're all here? In this little town? Are there *any* humans?"

She nodded. "About half the population. But we seem to be a magnet for the non-humans. We do everything we can to keep the town secret, but too many still find us all on their own. The town's always been that way, according to legend." She paused, and I sensed there was more, something she didn't want to, or maybe couldn't, say. "Hence, the reason for having to sign into the Registry. The Court wants to know who—and what—we have in town."

"And everyone gets along? Even with hunters?"

"Ha! Now that's funny." She fell silent for a moment, and the hum of the tattoo needle filled the silence. "We're *supposed* to. That's what the Court of the Sun and the Moon is for—to make sure everyone plays nicely together. But, as you can imagine, that doesn't always happen."

"Sounds like the sun has become the least of my worries. Hunters? Really?"

She chuckled. "Unless you lose control of your thirst, you don't need to worry about them. It really isn't so bad here. In fact, it's nice to be surrounded by some of your own. Maybe not everyone's exactly like you, but we *get* you. You'll see."

"A whole town of supernaturals. Wow." I shook my head as I tried to absorb it all. "This . . . this is kind of insane."

"This is Havenwood Falls. Welcome home."

CHAPTER 6

"**S**o do the humans know?" I asked as Addie dabbed at my tattoo with a tissue.

"Not most of them, but some do. Keeping the secret is paramount to our existence and the town's."

I nodded. "Same number one rule I learned when I first turned: protect the secret."

"Well, actually, around here, law number one is don't kill the humans." She stopped working and leaned over to look at me. "But that should have always been *your* number one rule."

I grimaced. "Um . . . not that I have, I almost did but was able to stop myself and it's most definitely a rule for myself, but, well, where I come from . . . some of the vampires just didn't give a shit. Said it was their right as a superior race. Not that I agreed with them or anything," I quickly added.

She rolled her eyes and snorted. "Damn vampires and their fucking arrogance."

"Hey!"

"Sorry. Not you. I know you wouldn't. Your kind *can't.* But some types are just . . . ugh. Some I just can't stand." She inhaled a deep breath, then said, "Okay, I need a moment."

She placed her palm against the fresh ink and closed her eyes as her lips moved. A warm tingling sensation entered my skin through the tattoo and spread into my blood and throughout my body.

She dropped her hand and opened her eyes. She smiled with an excited twinkle in her brown eyes. "It's done. And just in time."

She nodded toward the same set of French doors I'd come through at the back of the inn. The pitch black outside was no longer pitch black. I jumped up and rushed to the glass. The sky over the top of the eastern mountain was beginning to lighten.

"Oh, my god!" I threw open the doors and ran outside but barely stopped myself at the top of the porch steps, still under the cover of the roof, as I looked up.

Slowly the lighter blue bled into the darker hue of the night sky, and the few clouds glowed deep pinks and reds. It was beautiful, colorful, and full of promise of a fresh beginning. A second chance. A new day.

In a heartbeat, I was back inside.

How could I have been so stupid? So trusting? So naïve? I *knew* better! But I'd let my guard down, so eager to live in the daytime again.

"It's okay. It really works," Addie urged.

I spun and glared at her. "How stupid do you think I am? I don't even know you, what kind of person you are, or how you get your shits and grins. How do I know you're not trying to kill me?"

She flinched as though I'd slapped her, but watched me with steady eyes. "One day you will apologize for that. One day you'll see that it's like we've known each other forever. For now, you just have to trust me."

"Like that's gonna happen," I muttered. "Look, I have no idea what games you're playing and why, but I do know if there was a way for vamps to become day-walkers, they'd be all over this place. I don't care what your laws are. Vampires aren't exactly law-abiding citizens. There's no way in hell this would stay a secret."

I eyed my cottage through the glass doors and wondered if I could make it there without losing too many layers of skin. I had to get to safety and far away from this chick and her psychotic lies. Either she was delusional or she was a heartless bitch. But I was the fool, the dumbass who believed her childish stories of magic.

The back of my shoulder prickled and stung, a reminder of the tattoo, and heat coursed through my veins. A reminder of the magic? I shook my head. I couldn't fall for it. Again. Maybe that was the true secret ingredient of the ink—hallucinogens. This was Colorado, after all. Could have been cannabis oil in that bottle.

"You'll find out the truth soon enough," she said. "So just get it done with. Test it with a hand. Or, hell, even a finger. Surely you can recuperate from that if I'm lying?"

Nope. Not gonna happen.

"Oh, for shit's sake." She grabbed my arm and yanked me toward the doors. When I tried to fight back, an electric charge traveled through my body. I had no choice but to stumble along her side. "This is really stupid of me, but you've always preferred showing over telling, haven't you? Did you know there are only a few ways to kill a witch? And do you know what one of them is?"

"I'd sure like to find out," I snarled.

"A pissed off vampire," she said, and I tripped over my feet, startled that she'd tell me her weakness. Then I straightened, realizing what she meant, as we passed through the doors. "Of course, you have to be super fast, faster than I can cast off a spell, but it's been known to happen." She tugged me across the porch. "So, I've already provoked you and now I'm about to throw your ass out into the sun, which will hurt, and probably piss you off, right? But I know your specific type doesn't explode into flames right away, so I know there's time for you to do your worst on me. Yet, here I am. *Trusting* you. Because I know you won't do anything but thank me."

And with that, she shoved me down the stairs.

I stumbled a few steps onto the dormant lawn before catching myself. I was about to spin and attack—how the hell did she know so much and who did she think she was? But the light of dawn paralyzed me. As the realization that I wasn't sizzling and smoking settled in, I slowly lifted my gaze to the sky. My breath caught, trapped in my lungs, and I wasn't sure if I'd ever breathe again. *Is this really happening?*

The bright hues over the mountains lightened, and my heart rate went from 0 to 180 in an instant. A lump formed in my throat as tears welled in my eyes. Then, there it was. A bright yellow ball climbing over the jagged peaks, spilling its light down the mountainside and over the town like liquid gold. I gasped. My whole body trembled. And the tears spilled over. *This is really happening!*

I couldn't remember the last time I'd seen the sun rise. I'd rarely woken up early enough before, and by the time I knew what I was missing, it was too late. I clapped a hand over my mouth and the other over my still-racing heart as disbelief and awe for such beauty filled me.

When the orb finally made its full appearance over the ridge, I ran farther out on the lawn, threw my head back, and soaked in the sun as I spun in circles like a child. I thought I'd never again feel the kiss of the sun's rays without immediately blistering. I thought I'd live forever, yet never again be able to see the various blue shades above and the fluffiness of the clouds except through a window, peeking from behind the security of a blackout curtain. My heart swelled. The tears fell relentlessly, but laughter bubbled up and out as I continued spinning. Then I fell to my back on the grass and laughed hysterically while never taking my gaze from the sky.

I knew I was being watched, but assumed it was Addie. After another long moment, I reluctantly pulled my eyes from the sky and turned my head to see a large male body in the shadows. He leaned on his forearms against the railing as though he'd been there for a while. Had he been watching me? Our gazes locked, and I swore I could see something appreciative in his. A shiver ran through me, although I couldn't say if he caused it or the cold air did.

He cleared his throat. "She's asking for you."

Before I could respond, he turned and went back inside. Well, turned out he was just as cold as the air.

I didn't have to ask who "she" was. Addie sat on the porch steps, and there was only one other "she" who'd want to see me. I glanced up at the sky one more time and pinched myself. I'd spent years indoors or out only in the dark. I didn't want to go in yet. What if the spell broke? What if this temporary ink was really, *really* temporary? What if I'd been a fool treating Addie like I had and she rescinded her magic? What if this was my last chance to feel the sun caressing my skin? I didn't know it last time. This time I wanted to make the most of it.

"You can come outside any time you like," Addie said. "Now, do you have something to tell me?"

I sat up and looked at her, giving her a sheepish grin. "Thank you! Thank you, thank you, thank you!"

She nodded and grinned back. "And?"

"I'm sorry."

She shrugged and waved her ring-covered fingers, as though she hadn't practically demanded the apology. "Don't worry about it. You're not the first to call me a liar when it comes to this. In fact, I'd wondered what kind of stupid you were when you almost charged right out into the sun the moment you saw it. Now, come inside and take care of business, and I promise we can go to the park later as long as you wear a coat."

"I can't wait to tell Sindi," I nearly squealed as I sprang to my feet, partially out of excitement and partially in response to the way she'd spoken that last phrase, as though I was a small child with a new toy. That's exactly how I felt.

Addie's tone immediately flipped, becoming dark and harsh. "You have to wait."

I stopped at the bottom of the steps. "But—"

"Number two rule, remember?"

"But she's my best friend!" I didn't even mean to sound like a child now, but I heard the whine in my own voice.

Addie didn't respond at first, and I looked up at her expectantly. Sadness filled her expression. Her lips pressed together.

"She'll keep the secret," I promised. "I trust her more than anyone. She helped me when I needed her most. I can't possibly *not* tell her!"

Addie's throat worked as she swallowed. "Just . . . we have to follow certain protocol when we invite people to town. Even the tourists are handled a certain way. Otherwise . . . could you imagine all the supernaturals who'd swarm our town? And all the human lookie-loos? And then the carnage that would follow?"

The visions came clearly. I hadn't been making shit up before—every vampire in the world would be here if it meant seeing the sun again. And she'd said every supe gets inked, so they all gained something from it. I couldn't imagine how the others benefitted that could be as good as being a day-walking vampire, but it must have been just as life-changing.

I suddenly understood all of the secrecy and strangeness of the job offer, the scarce information available on the internet about Havenwood Falls, and the inconvenience of traveling here. They purposely made the town difficult to find.

"So why can't they all come, get the tattoo and leave? Or why don't you tell other witches about the spell or potion or whatever it is you use? There are other witches outside this town, right? Do you know how *valuable* this is?"

"Of course we do! And the reasons are nearly endless for not sharing, starting with the survival of humanity. There are wards on the town. Precautions in place. Limitations," Addie said as we headed inside.

"Such as?"

"Such as, the protection from the sun is only good while you're within the town's wards. If you go outside of town more than twenty-five miles, the tattoo vanishes and so does the magic."

"Well, that's good to know. No leaving town in the day or I fry."

"You can leave town. Just not the immediate area."

"Okay. 25 miles. Got it." We reached the lobby and began climbing the steps. "What else?"

My name came softly from Madame Luiza's room, and whatever else there was would have to wait.

"Michaela, dear," Madame Luiza whispered when I entered her room. My jaw ticked at hearing the wrong name again, but this time it was laced with a heavy accent, sounding more like Me-HAY-la. As I chose to not make a big deal of it as this elderly woman lay on her deathbed, it occurred to me that I must have reminded them all of someone named Michaela and having a similar name didn't help matters. Maybe she'd even worked here before, making it easy to slip up. Regardless, I sat on the bed next to her and took her outreached hand. "Listen to me, dear."

I nodded. "Of course. What can I do for you?"

"Just that. You can listen. Listen and not react. Because . . . I have much . . . to tell you." Her words paused as she struggled to simply breathe. I reached for her glass of water, but she shook her head. "Water won't help me now."

"It could make you more comfortable."

"I don't . . . have time . . . to be comfortable." She paused again to catch her breath, and I noticed little beads of sweat on her forehead. "You have a home here. You . . . always . . . have a home."

I gave her a small smile. "Please don't waste another ounce of energy worrying about me. I'll find another job. Another place to live."

"I *always* worry about you. You've always had a . . . special place." I thought she was losing her bearings again, but then she became completely lucid as her gray eyes hardened. "I mean it, Mehayla. This place . . . is yours. Take care . . . of it." Her voice faded, and her eyes began to drift closed, but she jerked herself out of it to pierce me with another hard look. "Take care of *them*. They don't know it, but they need you. And you need . . . them." Her gaze slid toward the door, as though she thought *they* might be standing there. Her voice came out softer when she spoke again. "You be careful . . . with those . . . Rocas. I know your heart . . . I know what it wants . . . but be wary, dear. They've gone . . . far . . . this time. But you . . . you are strong . . . you can change . . . everything."

I studied her face, trying to decipher anything of what she'd just said as her eyes fluttered closed and stayed that way. With her small hand still held between mine, I watched and waited for her to wake up again. A definitive peace spread over her face, slackening it, causing her mouth to curve into what appeared to be a secretive smile.

With soft steps, Addie came in and stood over us. She placed her palm against Madame Luiza's cheek and closed her eyes. When she reopened them a few moments later, they glistened. She bent over and kissed the old lady's forehead.

"Good night, Mammie," she whispered. "See you on the other side."

Addie must have heard the little gasp in my throat. She turned to me with a sad smile and gave my shoulder a squeeze. "It'll be soon, I'm sure. She's been hanging on for a long time, but now that you're here, she can go with peace. I need to go inform the Court. And don't worry. She's right. You always have a home here."

I returned her sad smile and nodded, then she left. Left me alone with a dying woman I barely knew and none of her own family around. Left me in an inn with nobody else to take care of it.

Left me to pick up the pieces, but to what I didn't know.

Madame Luiza never awoke. She drifted away peacefully the next night. I'd stayed by her side almost the entire time except to tend to guests—it turned out we did have a few—and to shower. When I'd returned from cleaning myself up, I could tell visitors had been in to see her. I'd only "met" Aurelia in passing that once, but I recognized her scent. Addie came and sat with us and was there when the old lady passed. I sensed Xandru nearby, too, lurking in the shadows. Others weren't far, but for some reason never came in.

Not until she was gone and Addie informed the Court.

Then suddenly people seemed to flood through the doors. Not knowing any of them and not wanting to deal with the awkwardness of being a stranger in such a personal situation, I slipped out to my cottage. I thought I heard my name whispered as I left, but figured they'd come get me if they needed my help. Nobody did for two days, and at first, I'd planned to stay holed up in my cottage until the commotion died down and I could slip away for good. But then I remembered the gift Addie had given me—the one Madame Luiza had insisted I receive right away—and I spent as much time outdoors during the day as I could.

I thought I'd explore the entire town, but simply standing at the inn's corner, the town square a diamond at this angle, sent tingles down my spine every time I saw something that felt familiar—which was pretty much everywhere I looked. Stores, restaurants, and bars lined three sides of the square, streets with parking separating them from the park setting at the center of town. A gazebo stood in the square's corner nearest to me, large and wooden with a round roof, nothing like the Bird Cage gazebo in Atlanta, but nonetheless I felt emotionally tied to it. A large, brick building lined the north side of the square, across from me, its clock tower pointing to the blue sky. It was clearly City Hall, but from here, tall pine trees blocked both buildings flanking it, yet I knew they were the Chamber of Commerce and the police station. *But how do I know?*

Forcing myself to keep going, I'd barely made it down one side of the square when the feelings became too much. The eerie sensations. The visions that popped in my head when I saw the Coffee Haven sign and the Shelf Indulgence storefront with a scene from *The Secret Garden* artfully displayed in the window. The ache of nostalgia in my heart when I stopped across from the middle of the square, staring down its bench-lined walkway to the fountain in the center. I somehow knew its sparkling interior came from real gold flakes in the paint, and I knew just as well that something significant had happened there. *But what?* And then there were the stares of people, strangers, as I passed by. Being out here no longer felt like freedom as the world seemed to be closing in on me.

I turned on my heel and hurried back toward the inn and the warmth and refuge of my cottage.

The next day I went east instead of west, away from the square, and found a large park in the corner of town, at the base of two mountains. It brought images of warmer days with music fests and movies in the park. At the far end was a trailhead that I followed a little ways up the mountain. But even in the middle of nature, with white aspen trunks and pine trees surrounding me and when I stood on the bank of the partially frozen river, I couldn't rid my mind of the visions. Couldn't dismiss the odd feeling that they weren't fiction created by imagination, but memories I hadn't known I'd possessed.

"This place is seriously fucking with me," I muttered to myself when I walked back into my cottage. "I should probably get out of here before I lose my sanity."

I restarted my fire and was warming my backside when there was a knock on my door. I found Addie on the other side.

"I don't know if you want to go or not, but the funeral is tomorrow," she said. "They're trying to beat this storm that's coming. I think she would have wanted you to be there."

Not until my feet carried me across town did I know if I was going or not. I followed a procession through a pretty cemetery to the back, then up a hill and through a stone-pillared passageway into another, separate and secluded area that appeared to be much older than the main section. We stopped in front of a stone building, where a man in a black suit placed an urn on a podium. I felt the bristle of Aurelia and the boy by her side who I assumed was Gabe, so I stayed back, huddled next to a large tree with my hat pulled tightly down over my ears. I could feel the colder air and smell the approaching storm Addie had mentioned. When the crowd cleared, I said my goodbyes silently as the funeral director took the urn inside what I presumed to be a columbarium.

As I walked across town back to the inn, I solidified my plans to figure out what needed to be done before I could pack up and return to Atlanta. I hoped Sindi wouldn't mind. I hadn't even been able to talk to her yet, once unable to find a good signal and the next time connecting to her voicemail. No internet at my cottage meant no email. I'd sent her a couple of texts, but she hadn't replied. Maybe she'd gone on with life, already forgetting about me. Maybe I wouldn't return to Atlanta with all of its memories and pain, after all, but would find a new place for a fresh start.

Which Havenwood Falls was supposed to have been.

But the longer I stayed here, the more I began to believe that it too contained many memories and much more pain. And even as I planned to leave, I also felt compelled to stay. One reason was to figure out the mystery of why Madame Luiza had taken to me so quickly and what she'd been trying to tell me with her last words. Were they irrational statements of a dying woman, or did she expend the last of her energy trying to tell me something?

And, hello, day-walking. I'd lose that as soon as I left.

Then there was the greatest pull keeping me here: the lone figure standing in front of my cottage when I returned, casually leaning against the post in a thick army-green coat over his formal funeral attire, with a look that made me want to undress right there and then. Fuck the cold.

"Everybody else thinks you're fragile and will break with what you need to know, but I know you better," Xandru said, and I could only nod because he was right. I didn't yet know how, but I couldn't deny the truth ringing through my soul: He knew me better than anyone.

CHAPTER 7

I couldn't breathe under the scrutiny of Xandru's piercing gray gaze as we stood motionless staring at each other. Everything about him was mesmerizing, from his high cheekbones and almond-shaped eyes to his square jaw and chin. Beautiful, yet too rugged to be called a pretty boy. The light color of his eyes was a bright contrast to his dark hair, dark brows and lashes, and olive skin tone. He looked like he hadn't shaved in days, considering the full beard growing in. And while his body was sculpted and chiseled perfectly, his posture always showed a confidence that could be perceived as threatening. Challenging.

But it wasn't the intense physicality that had seized me heart and soul.

Because the physical being in front of me was not quite what my heart and soul remembered, deep down, the memories, so faint I could barely grasp them, of a younger, less chiseled version. Except for the eyes. They were the giveaway. Especially now as they delved deep, reaching for those vague memories floating way back in the dark, and touching my soul. Showing me his. One I knew. Better than anyone.

He cleared his throat, breaking the connection. "Okay, then. I have a lot to show you. Come with me."

Blood flushed my face as I took that last phrase in more than one way, especially as he walked past me. I couldn't help but follow, if only to watch his powerful gait, the way his shoulders moved, his back muscles rippling under his white dress shirt . . . and that ass. Holy guacamole, what a fine ass. Jeans suited him better, but I didn't think I'd ever seen anyone make black dress pants look so good.

I followed him up the back steps and through the back doors of the inn. We headed toward the front, but instead of going all the way to the lobby, he opened a door and turned into the offices behind the front desk. We passed by a couple of free-standing desks and into the only closed-off room, in the back. I presumed it to be the owner's or manager's office.

"Here you go." He gestured toward the large, wood desk, which was covered with photos, some quite old and others recent, as well as a slew of papers.

My gaze immediately landed on a photo of me—albeit a younger version, dressed in snow pants and ski boots, goggles pushed up on my head and poles in my hand. There were others of me, as well, including one of a woman who looked like a slightly older version of myself, although that was impossible unless this town's weirdness also included time travel. I walked around the desk for a better look, picked it up and studied it, feeling an unexpected pang of longing for her.

"This must be Michaela," I murmured. No wonder people mixed me up with her. Similar names and nearly identical appearances. Only the coloring was a little different—her hair darker, her skin tone much lighter.

"Um, no," Xandru said. "That's Irina Petran."

I lifted my gaze to him, confused. "Why do I look so much like her?"

"She's your mother."

My eyes swept around the room, but not really seeing anything at all, my focus inward on the facts of my life. "Um . . . come again?"

"Irina Petran is your mother. That—" He pointed to a picture of a somewhat familiar looking man in another photo. "That's Mihail Petran, your father."

I shook my head. "I don't understand. These are the people who gave me up? Who left me in a dirty little town in Texas with complete strangers who didn't want me either?"

Xandru's brows scrunched together, forming two vertical lines between them. They smoothed out almost immediately. "Ah. I think that was the story they told you."

"Story? Who?"

"Irina and Mihail. Or, more accurately, whoever in the Luna Coven did the amnesia spell."

I threw the picture back down and cocked my head. "What the fuck are you talking about?"

He gnawed on his bottom lip and for a very brief moment, I was quite jealous of that lip. Or the teeth gnawing on it. I wasn't sure which. Then I came to my senses. I dropped my hands to my hips and tapped my foot.

"Nobody left you in Texas. You're not Kaela Peters. You're Michaela Petran, and you've always been here in Havenwood Falls, with your parents who loved you very much. So much that they gave up everything so you could go live a normal life and become the great doctor everyone believed you would be. The town's memory ward wipes away everyone's memories of Havenwood Falls once they leave—immediately for visitors and after a moon's cycle for residents—but they wanted to make sure your loss was thorough, that you forgot everything . . . every*one*." His voice caught, and he paused for a moment. "They gave you a history. A sad one, very far from here, that would keep you from ever wanting or even thinking about coming back here."

"In other words, they didn't want me," I whispered as I dropped into the chair behind the desk, my eyes roaming over all the pictures.

"That's not—"

I looked up at him. "Then why? Why would they send me away to never return and make me forget about them? I was just a child!"

"Because you're so fucking *special*." The sarcasm and anger dripped on the girl's last word as Aurelia showed herself in the doorway, her dark hair pulled up in a formal twist to go along with the black dress, sheer stockings, and heels she wore, making her look older than her behavior showed. Her brown eyes shot daggers at me. "And you weren't a child. You were a grown-ass adult."

"Aurelia," Xandru said as a warning.

She huffed out an annoyed breath with the expertise of a teenager and shifted her glare to him. "What is she even doing here, Xan? She shouldn't be here, and neither should you!"

"Someone has to do it," Xandru said. "And who else would it be? The coven's all tied up. My parents have no interest, and it's probably best to keep them away anyway. And you and Gabe are just kids. You can't take care of this."

"I'm not a kid!" she said petulantly as she crossed her arms over her chest and stuck her bottom lip out. I wondered if she'd stomp her foot next. "Everyone needs to stop treating me like one!"

Xandru turned, giving her the full force of his glare and that powerful stance. "We will when you stop acting like one. But you're sixteen, Aurelia. Don't rush it. Trust me. Being an adult isn't all that." He lifted his chin. "Now, if you care at all about your family, you'll stop acting like a brat and do what needs to be done. Otherwise, go back to the wake."

"Mingling with a bunch of adults giving me looks of pity and asking me how I'm holding up got old in the first five minutes."

"Get lost, Aurelia," Xandru said, in almost a growl.

She narrowed her dark eyes at him as her nostrils flared with each heavy breath she took. This girl had balls. I couldn't imagine standing up to Xandru at her age. Her eyes finally broke away and slipped to me before she spun on her heel.

"Fuck off, Xandru," she said under her breath, but I'd heard her. Xandru chuffed, clearly hearing her, too.

As he began to turn around, I had to brace myself, inhaling a slow breath, preparing for the inevitable shock-and-awe that always hit me when I saw his face. His eyes. They still pierced into me with the force of a laser—right to all my girl parts. I tried not to moan on my exhale.

"What did she mean?" I asked once I refocused.

His gaze found mine, and he immediately glanced away again as he pushed a hand through his hair, then rubbed it over his face. As though I unnerved him as much as he did me. His Adam's apple bobbed as he swallowed.

"You had just turned eighteen and graduated from high school," he said. "You'd been accepted to Emory University, which you'd been dreaming about attending since you were ten and read about one of their medical research studies. Considering who—*what*—you are, your parents had two choices: force you to give up the dream and stay here as part of the family and community, or allow you to go, reach your full potential, and live a normal life, but with no memory of them, of anything about your past."

"What do you mean, what I am? I wasn't *this* until a couple of years ago."

His stunning eyes slammed into me, nailed me to my seat. "Michaela, you've always been *this*."

"Uh, no. Regardless of what you say about my previous memories, I know the exact day I became a vampire. That is something I will *never* forget."

He nodded. "Trust me, I know. But you've always been moroi. At least, you've always had it in your blood."

My brows pulled together. "Moroi?"

"You really don't know any of this? Nobody told you about the moroi?" He blew out a breath when I shook my head. "It's the type of vampire we are—a mortal vampire. Have you ever met other vamps? You've noticed you're different?"

I hesitated before nodding.

"There are various kinds of what the mundane society, hell, even the covert world, refer to as vampires. We share similarities, but we also have differences. We, for example, are mortal. We're born human, but with a dominant vampire gene. If our gene is triggered and we turn, we live for hundreds of years, but we're not immortal. We can die of old age. Our hearts still beat, and if they stop, we die. And we can have children." He paused for effect. "The human way."

I flushed at his implication. He smirked.

"And you can still do that," he murmured with appreciation, and I felt like there was more meaning than I knew in that statement.

"Wait," I said. "Hold on. You're saying we and us. You're a moroi, too?"

He nodded. "A mature one, which means I've been turned."

My gaze dropped to the pictures. "And my parents?"

"They gave you the gene. It has to be triggered before age twenty-one."

"How?"

"You don't know how you were turned?" I shook my head again. "You don't know *who* turned you?"

"I know nothing. I didn't even know I was turned until I woke up with a killer thirst and almost killed my fiancé."

Something flickered in his eyes, but I couldn't determine what. A darkness. Perhaps a sadness or regret. He scratched his cheek before answering my question. "A moroi is turned by drinking the blood of another, mature moroi. Usually the parents provide their blood in a family ceremony because it strengthens the bond of the bloodline. The blood also passes extra powers and abilities from the source to the recipient."

"Powers and abilities?" I glanced back up at him and was immediately distracted, so I returned my gaze to the photos.

"The Romanian moroi originated from a sorcerer whose black magic backfired into him and his family. Ever since, the magic manifests in different ways when the gene is triggered. Usually something with the elements. It's basically a family trait, although there are stories of parents sometimes allowing another's blood to be given to their child if the source of that blood had a unique power or extra strong ability."

My brows dipped down as I studied one photo in particular, of the man and woman who were supposedly my parents. Who noticeably hadn't been around here. The question came out in barely more than a whisper. "And if it's not triggered by twenty-one?"

"The child goes on to live a completely normal, human life, able to marry a human, have children whose genes are dormant and don't need to be triggered, and grow old with their mates. And the moroi parents and the entire bloodline behind them . . . they die. As though their bodies slowly return to human, and their true age catches up, eventually killing them over time."

Unexpected tears blurred my vision, and I blinked several times to keep them at bay. "They're . . . gone?"

He didn't answer at first. He strode around the side of the desk, turned my chair, and dropped into a squat in front of me so he could look me in the eye. Trepidation filled his expression. "Your father passed a few years ago. Your mother a little over a year ago. And Mammie . . ."

"Madame Luiza?" I gasped.

"Your aunt."

My hand clamped over my mouth as my head shook. "No. This can't be true. It doesn't make sense. I don't even remember them!"

"Are you sure?"

My eyes closed as I inhaled a jagged breath. The visions I'd been trying so hard to repress since arriving in this town started pushing through. The sob escaped me.

"I wasn't turned in time! Why? *Why* would they do that?"

"They all wanted the best life for you, even knowing it would kill them."

I choked on another repressed sob. "Why couldn't I have that here? With them?"

He paused, and when I looked up at him, the trepidation was gone, now filled with sadness. "They believed Havenwood Falls, and the people here, were not the best life for you."

"I don't understand. This was *our* life. *My* life. Right? How could they think sending me away, forcing me to go off completely on my own, embedded with memories of a false past . . . how was that the best life for me? No family, no friends. If they wanted me to stay human, why couldn't I do that here? Or at least be able to come back, memories intact? *Life* intact?"

His eyes darkened, and he looked away. "They said it was too risky. You were more likely to be turned here. You'd *want* to be turned."

I didn't understand the problem. I mean, I wished I wasn't a vampire, but being a moroi sounded not quite as horrible—I could still have children, a dream I'd given up—especially if this really was my heritage. My family. And, more importantly, they'd still be alive. On the other hand, I knew too well that I'd never choose this life and the insatiable, murderous thirst that came with it, no matter how well controlled.

"Why would I do that?" I asked. "I mean, besides to save them, but obviously that was never a choice given to me. So why else would I choose to turn and give up the normal life they wanted for me? That I must have wanted so badly?"

His gaze came back to me, and our eyes collided. "For me."

I had no response. I could hardly think, especially the more intense his stare became. Capturing me. Swallowing me. Claiming me. My lungs began to burn and scream for air because I couldn't breathe, so lost in his gaze and his words and their meaning.

I gasped and broke the connection, turning away, looking everywhere but at him. A wave of emotions began to build—emotions I wasn't ready to take on yet. This was too much. All of it too much.

"I . . . I can't," I finally said on a soft breath as I stared at the desk in front of me. But the rest of the words, of what I wanted to say, failed to form, to come out. *I can't* applied to just about everything at the moment. I couldn't think, speak, and while I could probably feel, I really didn't want to.

Xandru blew out a harsh breath and stood. He walked back around the desk and turned. "Well, then, I can't either."

And with that, he strode out and away.

Finally able to breathe again, I sagged over with my elbows on the desk and my head in my hands. *What just happened?*

"Xandru?" Addie's voice came from the door that led back out to the lobby.

"I can't do this," he growled before the sound of his heavy footsteps carried across the wood floor of the lobby and out the door.

My fingers curled into my hair and rubbed into my temples as I drew in several breaths. Addie entered the room, but I didn't look up. Instead I stared at the contents of the desk under my elbows. A piece of bank stationery caught my eye, and my focus narrowed in on the letter.

"What the hell?" I straightened up and pulled the piece of paper out from under the photos, then read the full letter. Addie silently took off her coat, seeming not to mind that I hadn't acknowledged her yet. When I finished, I looked up as she tugged at her black miniskirt before sitting in the chair in front of me. She was sans glasses today, and her light brown hair was down, spread out over the shoulders of her gray blouse. I held the piece of paper up. "Do you know anything about this? Particularly this part right here?"

I pointed to the name Michaela Petran, which supposedly was mine. Which part of me had already come to accept was mine—the part that dared to acknowledge the visions that had been floating around my head for days as actual memories. My memories. Buried but returning from the grave.

"Hello to you, too." Addie gave the letter a quick read and shrugged. "It's a transfer of ownership of the inn to you."

"Obviously. But why?"

Her caramel brows lifted. "Because it's been in your family forever. You're the next in line. Why do you think Mammie worked so hard to get you back here? Aurelia and Gabe are certainly too young."

"Wait. What?"

"How much did Xan tell you?"

I blinked, then shook my head and waved a hand in the air, as though I could shoo away those last few minutes between him and me. "Obviously not everything. He told me who my parents were. That they're gone. That Madame Luiza was my aunt. That they didn't want to trigger my gene, even when it meant they'd die."

She nodded. "Your parents owned the inn. Mammie's been taking caring of it since they passed. As best as she could, anyway. Aurelia and Gabe, too . . . as best as she could. I think she'd been hanging on to wait for your return."

My chest tightened at the thought of Madame Luiza trying to do so much. Then Addie's meaning really sunk in. *And the hits keep on comin'.*

"Aurelia and Gabe . . . ?"

"Your sister and brother."

I sat back in my chair and blew out a long breath. That bratty little bitch was my sister? But I began to understand. "She hates me. And I can't blame her."

"She's a teenager. Remember when we were that age—oh, no, I guess you don't." She smiled sadly. "You will soon. For some people, the memories return as soon as they're back within the town's ward. For others, it takes time. And the spell they put on you was so strong. It may be a while."

"We were friends," I blurted. Although no memories of that had surfaced, I knew we had some kind of connection.

Her smile brightened a little. "Practically sisters. Besties forever." She sighed. "Until your parents decided forever was over for us. For you. And —" She looked over her shoulder, toward the door, and she didn't have to finish her thought.

"I'm not ready for that. For him." My eyes once again traveled over the desk. "There's just . . . so much."

I began sorting the photos into piles and the papers into a stack. Another letter from the bank caught my attention. And seriously. The shocks really wouldn't stop.

"Foreclosure?" I read the letter again, then let out a sad laugh. "Well, I guess I don't have to worry so much about the inn being mine. It won't be much longer."

My fingers released their hold on the letter and let it drift back to the desk. Addie snatched it up.

"This isn't right," she said as she read it. "We'll take care of this, Kales. They can't take this place from you, from your family. Something's going on here . . ."

I barely paid attention to the rest as the nickname made the tips of my ears tingle. Nobody in my recent past had ever called me that. It had always been Kae for short, or Sindi's occasional Kaekae. But I *remembered* that nickname. I remembered standing by the fountain in the square, gold flakes sparkling in the sun as Addie gave me a hug, and said, "Besties forever, Kales. Try not to forget me, okay?" And Xandru stood next to us, his hand on my lower back. And—

The sound of heavy and purposeful footsteps coming up the walk to the front door knifed into my recollection, severing it. I blinked and cocked my head.

"Oh, right. I came over to warn you," Addie said. "The wolves are descending."

"I'm sorry?"

"Sheriff Kasun and his deputies were on their way over to question you."

"For what?"

The front door opened.

"Um . . . for murder?"

CHAPTER 8

*K*aboom. The biggest bombshell of them all.

The little bell on the front desk dinged.

"*What?*" I gasped.

Addie cringed. "They found a body outside of town, in the woods. Looks like a vampire attack."

"And of course they immediately come to the new girl in town."

"You're not exactly new."

"Maybe not, but I wasn't a vampire the last time I was here, was I?"

The bell dinged again, several impatient times. I stood and exhaled a sharp breath. Like I needed this right now. My brain was spinning with information overload. I didn't even know if I could form a coherent answer to the simplest question, let alone ones that could put my freedom at risk—possibly my life. As I headed out of the office and toward the lobby, I realized I didn't have an alibi for much of my time here. In fact, most of it had been spent with a woman who's also now dead. Fabulous.

"Careful," Addie whispered as she walked behind me. "Wolves aren't exactly vampires' best friends."

I stopped in mid-step and hissed, "What does that mean?"

She bumped into me before catching herself. Her mouth was right by my ear as she explained in a low whisper. "They're wolf shifters. They always showed outward respect toward your father because of his seat on the Court, but the natural instinct to hate your kind runs deep."

Awesome.

Two men stood in the lobby, one in a khaki uniform with a deputy badge pinned to his chest and a brown felt hat in his hands, the older one in flannel and jeans. Both standing well over six-foot tall and with the same silvery-blue eyes and facial structure, they *had* to be related. Brothers, maybe.

The younger one bristled when he looked next to me, at Addie. "Came to warn her, did you?"

Addie gave him a warm grin, and her tone came out sickly sweet. "I came to make sure you do this properly, Deputy Kasun. She's entitled to a representative from the coven."

A noise almost like a growl rumbled in his throat, barely audible except to my keen ears.

"Ms. Petran," said the one who appeared to be in his mid-forties based on the laugh lines near his eyes and the speckles of gray around his temples and in the scruff along his jaw. While the cop seemed uptight and ready to pounce, this guy was more relaxed, his tone softer around the edges. "We're sorry about your aunt."

"Peters," I corrected. The deputy stiffened and peered at me with narrowed eyes. "That's what's on my ID, which I'm sure you want to see, right?"

"We already know it's fake," he said rather curtly, accusingly. As if *I'd* known it was fake. The older guy gave him a sideways look of warning.

"And thank you," I said to the older one. "Although, I just learned she was my aunt."

He nodded. "I'm Sheriff Ric Kasun. This is one of my deputies and son, Conall. We're aware of your background and understand this all must be rather strange for you."

"Strange would be putting it mildly."

"Doesn't matter what you remember from the past," Conall said, his demeanor in contrast with the sheriff's. Like they had a good cop–bad cop thing going on. Although, on closer inspection, while Ric's posture appeared more relaxed, his muscles were tense and his gaze swept subtly around the lobby, likely taking in every detail, ready to spring if he saw something he didn't like. "We need to know about last night. Where were you?"

"Care to be a little more specific with the time there, deputy?" Addie asked, her voice still dripping syrup, but with an underlying warning.

His upper lip twitched. "Between 4:25 and 5:12 a.m.," he bit out.

Addie snickered. "That's *very* specific. Russell's lap time?"

"Something like that," Sheriff Kasun said. "He found the body on his final run of the night out near Wylie's gulch."

"So where were you?" Conall snarled at me.

I pretended to think about it. "Pretty sure I was sleeping."

"At night?" he scoffed.

I couldn't help the small smile. "I've been working toward a more normal schedule, now that I can."

"When do you hunt?" he asked. "If you're on animal blood, as we've been told, best hunting is at night."

"You would know," Addie muttered. He ignored her.

"Madame Luiza provided me with more than a week's worth of bottled blood. I haven't needed to hunt yet. I don't know when I will, either. The bottled stuff here isn't too horrible, much better than anything I'd had before. And I kind of like animals. I don't like having to kill them." I paused. "Most anyway. The ones that don't wish me harm."

Conall cocked his head, sensing the challenge I might have been making.

"You have somebody to vouch for your whereabouts at that time?" the sheriff asked.

"That you were in bed," Conall clarified quite rudely.

And there was the question I knew would come. I tried not to take offense at the implication, although I'd been here less than a week. What kind of girl did he think I was? Oh, yeah. Murderer.

"I sleep alone," I said as nicely and calmly as I could muster.

"No need to be a dick, Conall," Addie said.

"We need to know if she has an alibi, Adelaide," Sheriff Kasun said to her. "That's well within procedure."

"Are you questioning all of the vampires?" she demanded.

"We will be. If we need to."

I blew out a breath, trying to release some of the tension that only continued to build. "Look, I get it. You have a dead body, and I'm the newbie here. You want to believe you know me, except you don't, because I'm not the old Michaela. But I'm not a murderer, either. I've never killed a human. I take pride in how well I control my needs. I swear I'm not the vampire you're looking for."

"In other words, you're barking up the wrong tree," Addie sniped, and I had to bite the inside of my cheek to keep from laughing.

"We do have empaths here in town," Conall said. "They'll know if you're lying."

I shrugged. "Bring them on."

"She's not lying," said a deep voice from behind me, sending stupid tingles down my spine. I couldn't even see him, but my whole body came on alert as he approached. "I'll vouch for her."

Oh, shit. What the hell was he doing? Barely more than an hour ago he was stomping away, acting like he wanted nothing to do with me. Now he was willing to lie on my behalf?

Conall looked over my shoulder, the disgust he felt obvious. "You were with her?" His nose wrinkled. "At least I know why she'd lie about it."

Xandru growled behind me. Seriously growled. The sound a vampire makes in warning. His hand suddenly appeared in my peripheral vision, pointing a finger at the deputy. "Show some respect, asshole."

Conall lifted a brow.

"To *her*," Xandru yelled, making me jump.

"Calm down," the sheriff quickly said, sensing the testosterone and who knew what other pheromones skyrocketing. "Both of you. Answer the question, Mr. Roca. Were you with her?"

I felt him bristle as he moved next to me.

"Not exactly," he said. "I was on her porch the whole night, though."

The sheriff squinted his eyes and cocked his head. "You were what?"

Xandru shifted next to me, sending heat over my skin. "I was watching her place."

"Watching or stalking?" Conall muttered, and the next thing I knew, Sheriff Kasun was breaking up a fight of an inhuman sort.

He stood between the two younger men, both of their chests heaving, more likely from adrenaline than needing to catch their breaths. Conall's eyes glowed a golden color, and Xandru's fangs were out. The sheriff stood there for a long moment, his arms out to keep them separated. When they seemed to have calmed down and gained control, he put his hands on his hips and turned to face Xandru.

"Why were you watching her place?" he asked.

The muscle of Xandru's jaw ticked. "You know why."

They stared hard at each other for a long moment. Something passed between them, but the sheriff seemed to let it go.

"Anyone see *you* out there?" Conall demanded.

Xandru turned his glare on him. "Russell did. And you also know why to that."

The two law officers continued their staring contest with Xandru. Another silent communication seemed to pass.

"Is this nonsense over?" Addie finally asked from my other side.

"Yes," Xandru said at the same time the other two said, "No."

"What else do you need from me, then?" I asked. "It's been a hell of a day, and I need a drink." Both pairs of silver-blue eyes cut over to me. "*Wine*. A glass of wine. Or a bottle. Sheesh."

"One more question," Conall said as he continued staring at me now. "What happened to Luiza Petran?"

Addie stepped forward. "All right, that's it. Now you really are just being a dick."

Xandru moved to her side, both of them in front of me now. "It's time for you to leave."

"Go on," Addie added. "Before I have to file an incident report to the Court."

"No worries, Adelaide," Sheriff Kasun said. "I think we'll be going over there ourselves."

With a final glare at all three of us, the men turned for the exit.

"I'd better go with them," Addie muttered quietly. She threw me a look over her shoulder before following them out the front door. And it wasn't until they were out of sight that I realized Xandru and I were alone.

He turned to face me, dropping his hands to his hips as his gaze traveled down my body and back up. I could hear his heartbeat change as he did so. Slowing at first, but then spiking again as his eyes studied my mouth.

"Why did you lie for me?" I asked.

His tongue swept over his lips, and I nearly forgot my own question, consumed by the desire to be that tongue. Those lips. "I didn't lie."

My gaze flew up to his eyes. I lifted a brow. "You were seriously on my porch all night? And I didn't know it?"

Those delicious lips curved into a smirk. "Vampire stealth."

I pointed to my ear. "Vampire hearing."

He lifted his chin. "You don't live in a town like this without learning a few extra tricks."

We stared at each other in silence, both of our hearts pounding. "Why then?"

He shrugged. "Maybe I like the view."

"So you were watching the inn?"

"Maybe."

I blew out a frustrated breath. "Can you give me a fucking straight answer? Finding out you were sitting on my porch all night last night without me knowing is a little damn unnerving."

"Every night. Since you've been here."

I pulled back. "What?"

"I've been around every night since you've been here."

"Watching the inn?"

"Yes. And your cottage."

"Why? And don't give me a vague non-answer about the view."

He hesitated, his eyes again doing that appreciative journey over my whole body. "Protecting you, Kales. Protecting the inn."

"From what?"

He chuckled. "All kinds of things. Them—the law. The Court. The bank. And the one committing those murders. I knew they'd come to you first, try to use you as a scapegoat."

"Whoa. Whoa. Whoa. You said murderssss. As in plural. They only mentioned one." I watched as Xandru pressed his lips together and rocked back on his heels. "You know something, don't you?"

"I *suspect* something. Yes."

"That you're not going to tell me?"

"Nope."

"Even though I could be in danger."

"You're not in danger as long as I'm around."

"Hmph. Well, that's the problem. You walked out today. How can I know or trust that you'll be around?"

He took two strides toward me, until we stood toe to toe. I had to tilt my head back to look up at him. He leaned down until his forehead nearly touched mine. His eyes locked onto mine, piercing into me, delving down, down, down, and I found myself leaning closer to him.

"I'm not the one who left," he said, his voice low, his breath fanning over my lips. The smell and the taste and the feel of him so close overcame my senses, making my body tremble and my knees weak. And my panties wet. But I held on to barely enough wherewithal to understand what he meant.

"It wasn't up to me," I said, and as soon as the words spilled from my lips, the memory of 18-year-old me in a fight with my parents rose to the forefront of my mind. I hadn't been given a choice to leave. I hadn't been asked what I really wanted—what I was really willing to sacrifice. Because it wasn't them. Not this life. Not Xandru. Memories of us growing up together, from when we were toddlers to our first kiss when I was in the fifth grade to how we were virtually inseparable throughout high school, even when he graduated two years before me. A clear vision of seeing him for the first time with gray-green eyes instead of blue, after being gone for a couple of weeks. And how, right after, my parents told me about my acceptance to Emory and that I'd be leaving in two days. "You were right. I would have chosen to be turned. And to stay. With you."

Our eyes held each other's, and old feelings began to push against the barriers, what I could feel was about to become an avalanche. Before they overwhelmed me, sucked me under, buried me, I pushed up and against him and crashed my mouth against his.

His hands immediately came to my face, cradling it and holding tight. Mine slipped up, into thick, soft hair. The kiss deepened, our lips parted, our tongues met. And not for the first time, I knew. In fact, the moment mixed with the memory of the last time. The urgency, the passion, the desperation of saying goodbye, but now we were saying hello again. I missed you. I want and need you now more than ever. With just as much urgency and passion and desperation.

His mouth was delightful. His kisses delicious, sending a ping straight through my core. I sucked on his bottom lip, and he returned the favor, eliciting a whimper from me. He groaned in response, then suddenly pulled way. I nearly fell forward at his sudden absence, and I gasped for more while staring at him halfway across the room.

"What?" I asked.

"There's something I don't get, Kales." Xandru's gray-green eyes suddenly turned hard. Angry. Accusing.

"What?" I repeated.

"How could you forget me so easily? Forget us? After everything we'd been through?"

CHAPTER 9

J stared at him, panting, my brain muddled.

"You promised our love would conquer the amnesia spell," he said.

"You promised you'd follow me to the ends of the earth," I countered. I didn't know I knew that until I said it, but then the memory of our last moments together floated through my mind.

"And I did."

"Uh, pretty sure you didn't. I was there. You're still here . . ."

He ran a hand through his hair, causing the top to fall forward over his temples. "I did go to Atlanta. I wasn't supposed to. I'd sworn to the Court I wouldn't interfere. But fuck, Kales. I couldn't do it anymore. It hurt too much. I was fucking up all over the place, contributing to the Roca reputation when I'd promised you I never would. I had to find you."

My heart pounded at this revelation. "Did . . . you? Find me?"

Pain filled his eyes, overflowed into his entire expression and stature. But only for a moment. He quickly straightened up to his full height, lifted his chin, and hardened his eyes again.

"Yeah, I did. And you were so fucking happy. Taking your classes. Making friends. Dating some pretty-boy asshole."

I sucked in a breath, imagining him seeing me with Ryan and Heather, when they were both mine, not each other's. "When was this?"

He threw his hands up. "A few times over the years. I don't know what I was thinking. I was a fucking masochist, I guess. Because the first time was hard. You'd only been gone a few months. And I was nothing to you. Not even a vague memory. You looked right at me that time, and not a hint of recognition. I realized they were right. That was the best life for you, and I needed to leave you alone."

Pain filled his voice, mixed with resolve.

"But for some dumb ass reason," he continued, "I went back again. And again. Hoping maybe something changed with you, especially after you turned. I would have taken just a flicker of familiarity in your eyes. But there was still none. I finally had no choice but to accept that you were truly gone. That you really had forgotten me, everything we'd been through, the life we'd had planned. That you'd moved on to a better one. And while it killed me, I was happy that you were happy."

Silence fell over us as we stared at each other. I knew exactly how he'd felt—the same way I'd felt with Ryan and Heather. Except not quite. For one, what Xandru and I had was so much more intense than Ryan's and my relationship. So much more real. Although I couldn't remember every detail of our relationship, I could feel that fact in my bones. In my soul. The relationship Ryan and I had, the one I'd thought was my epic, forever love, was superficial in comparison. And for two . . .

"I didn't forget you," I whispered. His brow shot up. I took a few slow steps closer to him. "Some part of me didn't let go. I was confused. Maybe because of the spell or whatever. But there were things I'd attached to Ryan that didn't belong. And, I don't know, maybe that's why I attacked him, because the very basal part of me knew he wasn't mine. I wasn't his. Because I already belonged to someone else. Someone my subconscious has never completely let go."

He cocked his head. I moved a few more steps toward him, close enough to lift my hand to his face. He leaned into my palm as my thumb swept over his cheekbone.

"These eyes, for example," I said quietly. "They've haunted my dreams for years."

His hand grabbed mine, but I took control and brought his knuckles across my lips, along my jaw.

"These hands," I continued. "They touched me almost every night."

He exhaled heavily, slowly. "Could have been anyone's hands. You could have been dreaming about anyone. Pretty boy, for example."

I tilted my head. "Did I mention the eyes? You do know nobody has eyes like yours."

He dropped his chin and looked at me through his lashes. "They're moroi eyes. *You* have eyes like mine."

"Nope. Not exactly the same. Similar, but . . . I know your eyes, Xandru. Maybe I couldn't grasp the memory of who they belonged to, but I lost myself in them every night. And besides." I undid the top buttons of his dress shirt and slid my hand underneath it, slowly pulling it to the side while cherishing the feel of the heat of his skin against my palm. "I have never forgotten this."

"My birthmark? You remembered that?"

"Who could forget a birthmark shaped like a duck?" I smiled as I glanced down at the skin over his heart. My fingertip traced over the mark as I slowly looked back up at him.

"Dragon. How many times have I told you, it looks like a dragon?"

"Nope. I still see a duck." Both of our lips curled up for a moment as we gazed at each other. "I'm sorry—"

My apology was cut off when his mouth slammed down on mine.

The kiss started as though he searched for something, his eyes open, piercing deep into mine while his lips and tongue explored. I held his gaze while kissing him back, and he must have found what he wanted, needed. With a growl, he lifted me, and as he started walking, I had no choice but to wrap my legs around his waist. He carried me up the stairs and to an empty guest room, kicking the door shut behind us, our lips never separating the entire time.

But now he let go, setting me back on my feet. His eyes raked over me, sending a shiver down my spine with their heat.

"Are you sure about this?" he asked, his voice husky. "Because I've been waiting a fucking long time for it. But I need to know you want this. That you're in. For good this time."

"I'm in, Xandru. My heart, my soul, they've always been in. My brain just didn't know it."

He studied my face as he stalked toward me, forcing me to back up until my knees hit the bed. But just before I was about to plop on my ass, he swooped me up, spun us, and sat on the edge of the bed with me straddling him, my skirt bunched up around my hips. And with only my cotton panties and his dress pants between us, I could feel with all certainty just how much he wanted this. His hand slid up my back and into my hair, cradling my head, while the other splayed out over my lower back and pulled me against him. I grasped his shoulders as my breasts pressed into his chest, my hips rocked, and the friction brought out moans from both of us.

Our mouths moved together in perfect sync, pressing and sucking, parting and tasting. When his left mine, I whimpered, but then he pulled on my hair, tugging my head back, lifting my throat to his lips. His open mouth skated over my jaw and down my neck, his tongue swirling against my skin, sending webs of pleasure everywhere. He paused at my carotid, first licking the thick, pulsing vein, then sucking on it. Pleasure shot all the way to my core.

"Oh my god," I breathed as I pushed down on his lap and rocked again, needing to feel the pressure between my legs. "Do that again."

He paused, and his eyes rolled up to look at me through those thick, dark lashes. "You've never fucked a vampire before?"

I scowled. "I never fuck anyone and tell."

He smirked, knowing my answer already. "Get ready then. I'm about to—"

"If you say rock my world, I am so out of here."

His eyes darkened for a brief moment, but then he laughed. Who knew that sound would be a total turn on? When I reacted with another shift of my hips, rubbing my center against his erection, his eyes darkened in a very different way.

"I was going to say," he said huskily, "I'm about to show you one of the best parts of what we are."

His fangs let out right before he leaned into my throat again, licking and sucking at my vein, the tips of his fangs scraping across my skin. At the same time, his hand slid from my back, over my ribs, and to my breast. He cupped it for a moment, the heat of his palm making my shirt and bra feel nonexistent. His hand expertly teased my breast, the friction causing my nipple to pebble against his palm while his mouth never left that spot on my throat. I arched back more, rocking in a quickening rhythm, rubbing my clit against his hard-on at the same pace his tongue assaulted me. He rolled my nipple between his thumb and forefinger before giving it a hard pinch, making me cry out with pleasurable pain. Then his hand traveled southward, over my stomach, down in between us, slipping into my panties.

"Oh, fuck, you're so wet," he said against my throat. His fingers stroked my folds before finding the swollen bundle of nerves aching for his touch. He barely grazed it, and I cried out again. His thumb pressed into it, swirled over it as his fingers slid to my opening. "Get ready, Kales. It's like nothing else."

His lips clamped onto my throat and sucked, then his fangs dug in at the same time his fingers slid into me. I came undone. Completely. Fucking. Undone. And I couldn't stop coming undone as his fingers stroked and his mouth sucked. I lost all control as my back arched and my hips rolled on their own, fucking his fingers while he drank my blood. And just when I didn't think I could climb any further, his thumb pressed against my clit, my entire body clenched around him, and I screamed his name as I soared.

"Oh god," I finally breathed as I started to come down.

"Not the first time I've been called that."

The deep voice, as sexy as it was, cut into my bliss. His tongue slid over his bottom lip, licking my blood off it. I touched a finger to my throat, but of course the wounds had already healed. The smell of myself all over him, the way I'd just lost control . . . heat exploded in my cheeks. He smirked.

"You're fucking beautiful," he said as his hand slipped out from me. He lifted it to his mouth and sucked on his fingers. "I'm not sure what tastes better, though—your blood or your pussy."

I might have come again just from his dirty words.

"Should I get a better taste?" he asked. Before I could respond, he flipped us over, and I found myself on my back, my ass on the edge of the bed, and Xandru between my legs. He leaned his head down.

"No," I gasped.

He froze. "No?"

"I want you inside me. *You.*"

He gave me a sexy grin. "Say what you really want, Kales. Talk dirty to me."

I shook my head. "Not now, Xan. I don't want to fuck, I want to make love. It's . . . it's been so long."

He stared at me for a long moment, then his beautiful eyes fell closed. He exhaled a long, slow breath. But otherwise didn't move. I leaned up on my elbows, waiting. Then he stood up.

"You're right," he said as he started pulling my skirt down over my thighs.

"Um . . . I'm not sure if you heard me right. I *want* you. Now. But *all* of you. Your whole being, not just your cock."

He leaned in and pressed his lips to my ear. "I know. I do understand.

And this is not how it should be. Not our first time . . . our new first time. You deserve better."

His mouth moved to my mine and delivered a delicious but tame kiss.

"You misunderstand," I said against his lips.

"No, but you have to stop." His fingers wrapped around my wrist as I moved my hand down his stomach. "Or I won't be able to."

"Then don't. I don't want to stop."

"I do."

I stilled in his grasp, only inches from stroking him. "Let me take care of you at least."

"Ah, Michaela, you already did. Watching you come like that . . . something I never thought I'd do again. And drinking your blood while you did—it was my own personal heaven." He tugged on my wrist, pulling me to my feet. "There will be lots of time to take care of me, yeah?"

I straightened out my clothes. "Yeah. Plenty of time for us both."

"You're staying then?"

I glanced around the guest room, my gaze pausing at the window and the view of the mountains, before coming to his face, nearly as impressive. "Where else would I go?"

He leaned toward me as though to kiss me, but his pocket buzzed. He retrieved his phone, glanced at the screen, and swore under his breath. His entire demeanor changed.

"I have to go, but I'll be back later. We have a lot to talk about."

When he didn't come back, I began to wonder what kind of fool I was, thinking I wouldn't be given a taste of my own medicine.

CHAPTER 10

$\mathcal{T}$he snowstorm hit, forcing me to spend a few days inside. I spent a lot of time admiring the beauty of the freshly fallen snow on the mountains and the trees, and the rest learning about the business side of the inn. I seemed to know the inn itself quite well, as though I'd grown up in it, which, I began to recall, I basically had. Checking guests in and out also came as second nature, and apparently nothing had changed since I'd worked the front desk all through high school. I only had a few guests come and go, and once I learned how to use the ancient reservation system, I understood why the inn was in such disrepair and being threatened with foreclosure. The low revenues couldn't possibly pay the utility bills for this huge manor, let alone any other expenses.

"There's just no way," I said on a sad sigh as I sat behind the desk in the back office. I'd cleaned it off, set the photos to the side, and organized all of the papers that had been covering it. Then I studied everything I could find in the files. None of it good news.

"No way what?" a female asked from the doorway.

I looked up to find Addie standing there in jeans and a black hoodie with a big silver eye on it, her coat folded over her arm.

"No way this place can stay in business." I gestured toward the bills and bank statements spread out in front of me. "From my calculations, we need at least a fifty-percent occupancy rate to break even, and we haven't had that in over a year."

"Probably not since your mother died." Addie came in and took a seat in one of the chairs on the opposite side of the desk. "Mammie didn't really know much about managing this inn. Business was never her forte. She was spectacular at making people feel at home, but she didn't know how to get them here in the first place."

I frowned at the papers in front of me. "It got worse with her, but honestly, it started years ago. Five years ago this fall, to be exact." I looked up at her. "My father was the businessman, right? Is that when he . . . passed?"

She tilted her head as she briefly thought about it. "Erm, he wouldn't have even started aging yet. You wouldn't have passed the age of maturity, so he would have been fine." She gnawed on her lip for a moment. "I think I know why, though. A couple things, actually. First, your mom was pretty depressed after you left. She'd been part of the decision, as far as I know, but that didn't mean she liked it. Everyone noticed a change in her. So your dad was dealing with a lot. And then, well . . ."

"Well, what?" I asked when she didn't continue.

"You might get mad."

"Why?"

"Well, that's about the time Tase Roca bought the ski resort and started expanding it."

I folded my hands on the desk. "I don't get it. Why would I be mad?"

"His first phase of expansion was adding a few cabins right at the bottom of the mountain. Ski-in/ski-out kind of places."

At the mention of skiing, all sorts of memories flooded my mind. Visions of us on the slopes, skiing when we were younger and then snowboarding. Racing each other because most of the guys our age couldn't keep up or didn't dare do the moguls like we did.

"Do you still ski?" I asked excitedly.

She blinked at the unexpected change in conversation. "Uh, yeah. Love to. So did you—wait. Do you remember something?"

"I do! You and me killing it on the slopes. I can't wait to go again!" I nearly squealed.

She laughed. "We had a lot of fun out there."

Her expression fell, though.

"What?" I asked. "Please don't tell me it's not the same."

"Well, it's not that. I mean, it's not quite the same because we have more tourists coming in than we used to."

I glanced at the papers on the desk. "More tourists, but fewer guests?"

"That's the thing. Like I said, Tase bought the resort and started expanding it."

"With a few cabins."

"At first, yeah. Then over the next few years, he added a second ski lift, a couple of new trails, more cabins . . . The growth was slow at first, but then it kind of exploded two years ago. The Court wasn't happy about it, but they do like the extra money flowing in."

"Obviously not to here. Isn't the Whisper Falls Inn the largest hotel in town?"

She nodded.

"But the least busy." That wasn't a question.

"Besides the cabins at the resort, there have been other places popping up. A couple of B&Bs. The Green Coven even bought up a bunch of the townhomes and condos and rent them out by the week. We've been working overtime, the Luna Coven that is, to ensure the wards stay intact and everything remains under control. They had to pull the reins in on Tase. He's been flipping out lately because of it."

"Tase? You said Roca?"

She picked at her sleeve. "Yeah. Xandru's older brother."

Something was off in her tone. My eyes widened as I remembered.

"You still have a crush on him! Oh my god. Are you *with* him now?"

"Uh, *no*. Not really, anyway. I don't think anyone will ever nail that man down." Her rings glinted in the light as she waved her hand in the air as though dismissing him. "I don't want to talk about that. He's an ass most of the time. Especially lately."

I dropped my chin in my hand. "So Tase's business ventures are responsible for the Whisper Falls' demise."

"Bottom line? I think so."

I gnawed on my lip. "Does Xandru have anything to do with it?"

She became completely engrossed with her sleeve again.

"Ah. This is where I get mad," I said as realization set in. After everything he'd said about protecting the inn and me, come to find out he'd played some kind of role in the inn's sad state. "He did, didn't he?"

"They keep everything close to the vest, but I think it's a family affair. I don't really know how deep for Xan, though. He's always done his own thing, but when you left . . . he pretty much lost it, Kales. Adrian, Andrei, and Tase were all he had."

My mind conjured forth vague recollections of faces obviously related to

Xandru as she ticked off the names. His brothers. The entire family had somewhat of a bad reputation in town, but I'd always thought if given the chance, they'd do the right thing. I supposed I'd expected them to live up to Xandru's standards. Apparently, they'd brought him down to theirs.

Then something else occurred to me.

"Holy shit. Maybe Xandru's so damn interested in keeping an eye on the inn because they plan to buy it! Have the Rocas ever mentioned that?"

She pulled a face and squirmed in her chair. "Well . . . they *have* held a grudge against your family for a very long time. I don't know all the reasoning behind it, but I do know everyone in town practically worshipped your father and your family, while the Rocas were always treated differently."

"Maybe because they have a bad reputation?"

"Or maybe they earned the reputation because they got tired of being treated like shit for a hundred or so years."

"And now they found a way to screw my family over. I can't believe I let him—" I cut myself off.

Addie's eyes sparked with curiosity as she leaned forward. "Let him what, Kales? What did you let Xandru do to you?"

She said it as though she knew exactly what he'd done to me, causing blood to rush to my cheeks. Which made me even madder.

"I can't believe I let him play me! He totally fucking played me."

Realizing I wouldn't dish out any more details than that, she sat back in her seat. "Don't jump to conclusions yet. The Rocas . . . they're complicated. If you remembered everything, you'd know that. And Xandru most of all."

I nodded. "I do remember that. But at least you had a pretty good idea of what you were getting into with Tase. You *wanted* the bad boy. I'd always thought Xan was different, though. But I guess he changed. Or maybe I was wrong from the beginning. Maybe he and I were wrong, together."

"Kales, you don't really believe that, do you?"

I shrugged. I didn't know what to believe anymore. Not when it came to Xandru.

"At least give him a chance to explain. Talk to him."

"That'd be a lot easier if he didn't disappear right after . . . *playing* me."

She giggled at the innuendo, and my anger diffused.

"Like a fiddle?" she teased.

"More like an electric guitar," I quipped. "And I sang like a damn rock star."

Her eyes popped open wide, and we both fell into a fit of laughter.

"Well," I said once I regained control. I lifted my chin and squared my shoulders. "I'm not giving in yet. I don't know how, but I'll find a way to save this inn. The Rocas—or anyone else who's trying to get their hands on it—can fuck off."

She grinned. "That's the spirit! But can you start tomorrow?"

I pointed at the letter from the bank. "I have 32 days to come up with a payment plan."

"Good. So you can start tomorrow. Come on. I have some time off." She stood up. "You've been avoiding a few things—some important people —and I think it's time you got reacquainted."

"I don't know," I said slowly.

She was right. I'd been avoiding everything and everyone as much as possible. I hadn't exactly been welcomed back with open arms, but there had been a lot of staring. I guess I couldn't blame anyone, considering I wasn't supposed to ever come back and especially not with a blood thirst, there was a death in my family the third night after I returned, and shortly after, I was accused of murdering someone else.

"The longer you stay holed up in here, the more they're going to stare when you do finally come out. Just rip the Band-Aid off already."

"Ugh!" She was right. I glared at her with her smug grin. "I hate you, Bratty Addie."

She laughed and then rushed at me with her arms open, slamming into me with a hug. "There's my girl! I've missed you."

Feeling her arms around me, smelling her so very familiar scent, I sighed with content. Everything I felt about Xandru was all mixed up now, but Addie truly did feel like home.

The bright sun and blue sky were deceiving, because the air remained cold. The snow had been cleared from the roads and sidewalks, but still blanketed the grass and rooftops. Bundled in coats, knit hats, and gloves, we walked to the town square, getting as far as Coffee Haven before we stopped for hot coffee and a late breakfast. The scent of freshly baked pastries and java beans immediately cued my memories, and I noticed the shop had changed somewhat from what I vaguely remembered about it, with more plants and paintings and drawings hanging on the walls. Addie credited Aster McCabe, who caught us up on the local rumors about the recent murders.

Aster was a couple of years younger than us, always quiet and a bit of a loner, while her sister Reeve, who'd been in our class, had been the perfect little doll that Addie and I not-so-secretly made fun of. Mostly because Reeve and I were always pitted against each other in every possible way—GPAs and test scores, homecoming and prom royalty, cheerleading . . . she especially hated me on the slopes because I was as good as her although I was human then and she never was. I'd love to race her now. But she'd left town, and here was Aster, managing the coffee shop like a boss. And dude, could she make an amazing blueberry scone.

"See? That wasn't so bad, was it?" Addie asked as we crossed the street to the park area of town square.

A blue pickup on the far side caught my attention. "Hey, isn't that Xandru's truck?"

Addie followed my gaze. "Yeah, it is."

Xandru and another guy who looked remarkably similar to him—Tase, I thought—walked up to it and opened the doors. He looked over at us, obviously hearing his name. I waved for him to wait. He shook his head before they both slid in the truck and took off.

"Well, what the hell was that?" I asked.

Addie waved her gloved hand in the air. "That was typical Roca. They're always like that."

My coat pocket buzzed with a text message notification. Hoping it was Sindi, I retrieved my phone, only to find a curt message from Xandru: "Talk later. Promise."

Maybe I don't want to talk to you, I thought with a scowl as I shoved my phone back in my pocket and continued strolling with Addie.

I stopped us at the fountain, remembering my last day here and saying goodbye to Addie and Xandru. Although I'd known what was about to happen—whatever the town's memory ward didn't wipe out when I left, the coven's spell would make sure I forgot forever—but I hadn't believed it'd be as thorough as they'd promised. I'd held onto the hope that some part of me would remember, that I couldn't possibly forget the lifelong friendship Addie and I had or the epic, deep love Xandru and I shared. They'd called it puppy love, young love, a high school crush. He and I had always known it was so much more than that. And my parents had, too. He was one of the reasons they'd wanted me to leave.

Maybe they'd been right all along.

"You're getting sad on me," Addie said. "Come on."

She slipped her arm around mine and tugged me past benches and old-fashioned lamp posts toward the south side of the square as the clock on City Hall's tower began to dong in the next hour. Children ran around us, laughing and screaming as they threw snowballs at each other.

"Let's stop for a visit with Madame Tahini so you can access the residents part of the website," Addie said as we approached a storefront with Euro-Asian style writing on it. As soon as I saw her, I remembered the strange little woman known around town as Teeny Weeny Tahini. Besides giving readings and whatever else she did in her weird little shop that smelled like a complex concoction of herbs, she was the keeper of the website's password.

"Make sure you have her number and know her hours," Addie said once we left. "She changes the password like every 26 ¾ hours. I think just to mess with us."

"Why is she the one in charge of it? She's not even affiliated with the website. Does she even know how to use the internet?"

Addie laughed. "Who knows? This is Havenwood Falls. Not a lot makes sense."

We left town square and the main business district, passed City Hall, and entered the residential area as we headed north up Eighth Street. As the street began to slope steeply upward, we came to a gate that crossed the road, with a fancy metal sign that said Havenwood Heights.

"The sign looks different than I remember," I commented.

"The Rocas redid it," Addie said. Right. Mr. Roca had a metalworking shop. My memories were slowly returning in the weirdest ways.

Addie flicked her fingers and murmured something, and the gate began to roll open. I could hear the waterfalls nearby, a whisper of a sound in town on a quiet night, but a muffled roar out here. Something dark poked my mind as we passed through the gate.

I grabbed Addie's arm. "I don't know about this."

"It's time, Kales. Band-Aid, remember?"

I exhaled sharply and followed her up the steep incline. We passed an enormous house on the right, then a road on the left. Addie's family owned two of the mansions at the end of that cul-de-sac, but we weren't going to Addie's house. We kept on up the mountain road, passing by woods of aspen and evergreens that separated the large estates, tendrils of mist from the falls rising above them. The late winter sun beat down on us, and for the first time since I'd arrived, I could actually feel its warmth. If I were human, my legs would have been rubber by now from the climb. As it was, I struggled to breathe properly, still adapting to the thin atmosphere. But the closer we came, the more I was drawn to the estate like a magnet. I smelled home. I tasted it. I felt it.

When it finally came into view, though, my heart dropped.

What had once been a magnificent manor on the right side of the upper cul-de-sac was now not much better off than the inn. While the inn was a Victorian style built during the first days of the town in the 1850s, our house was quite newer but with an older, gothic style to it. Mom had said it made her feel more at home—as in Romania home. I swallowed against the lump that formed in my throat when I realized I'd just thought of her as *Mom*.

We walked up the long sidewalk to the front door, where loud rap music blared behind it. Addie gave me a surprised look as she threw open the door with a twist of her hand. The music cut off immediately. We walked inside, into a grand foyer with marble floors and a double curving staircase of wood and intricately detailed wrought iron. More Roca handiwork. A layer of dust covered the bannister and the table that sat in the middle (I remembered fresh-cut flowers in vases were usually there in the spring and summer), and wallpaper that had once been elegant and luxurious curled and lifted at the edges.

"Aurelia!" Addie yelled, her voice echoing off the marble floors. The girl ran from one of the upstairs hallways to the balcony above us. "You're supposed to be at home at my place. Or at Lena's. What the hell are you doing here?"

"Lena had shit to do. And *this* is my home, not yours! What the hell is *she* doing here?"

The boy I'd seen with her at the cemetery came out from the same direction she'd come from. From their rooms, I recalled. My bedroom had also been down that hallway, at the end of the wing. He had the same color hair as mine, not quite as dark as Mom's and Aurelia's, but with the same brown eyes as our sister—the same brown mine had been before I'd turned. He was thin and awkward looking, like all twelve-year-old boys. He simply scowled at me, but didn't say a word.

"She has every right to be here," Addie said.

"She has *no* right!" Aurelia screamed.

"Her name is now on the deed," Addie countered.

Aurelia seethed, her nostrils flaring as she glared at me. "That is so unfair! Two more years and it would have been mine." Her eyes narrowed, shooting daggers at me. "What did you *do* to them? They weren't supposed to go so soon!"

"Aurelia," Addie warned with a kind voice.

"Just leave me alone!" She ran off, back to her room.

Gabe still stood there, staring at me. "You shouldn't have come back," he said flatly before turning and disappearing down the hallway.

"They blame me," I said, my shoulders dropping.

"They were too young to understand."

"Why would our parents do that to them, though? To all of us? The hell with being too young. *I* don't understand."

"Well, she's right. They did go too soon. It wasn't supposed to be that quick. They should have had at least another ten years, maybe longer. Long enough for those two to grow up and begin their own lives."

"Away from here?"

"I think that was the plan."

"But everything got messed up."

"Yep. Goddess always has Her own plans."

I crossed the foyer to the formal living room to our left, where all of the furniture was draped with protective covers, and walked over to the big picture windows lining two walls. Out one side was the spectacular view of the town spreading out below, looking like it belonged on the front of a Christmas card. The City Hall's clock tower and a couple of church steeples stood up like sentinels over the town. The sun was nearly straight overhead, its rays blinding as they bounced off the snowy roofs and lawns. Across town, the ski lifts climbed the mountainside, and skiers carved their way down the slopes.

"Maybe we'll get another snow this season to go," Addie said from my side. "We can go up in the summer now, too. There's a lookout with a snack shop at the top of the mountain over there. One of Tase's new additions. He's planning to add a slide and other things for the summer tourists next year. Eventually a restaurant."

"Good for him," I muttered as I turned to the other wall.

Although the view of town was beautiful, this one was breathtaking. Another mansion sat across the cul-de-sac, most of it blocked by evergreens. But beyond it was an upper portion of the falls. From here, they appeared to shoot out the side of a rock wall and free fall into the trees below. Right now, they were partially frozen over, cascades of ice that created an incredible work of art by Mother Nature herself. That explained why the roar had been muffled. In summer and close-up, the sound was nearly deafening.

I couldn't see it from here, but I remembered what looked like a large log cabin at the top of the falls, but was a tavern owned by the Alversons. Lena Alverson was one of Aurelia's good friends. I also recalled a pool at the bottom of the mountain that the falls poured into, surrounded by boulders and trees. During the warmer months, a great mist rose from the pool enshrouding the area with a magical feel. And if memory served me right— which it was starting to do—the pool fed a stream that crossed town and fed into Mathews River, which carved its way along the base of the south mountain. Tears stung my eyes as I remembered standing here with Mom, who loved those falls so much.

"So, uh, what do you want to do?" Addie asked from behind me.

I swiped at my eyes with the backs of my hands before turning, and then I looked around the room before my gaze rested on her face. I shrugged.

"I don't know. It's home, but it's weird."

She gave me a sad smile. "I figured it would be, but thought it'd help with the memories."

"It has." I glanced around again. "It just feels different. Without them."

"I'm sure the covered furniture doesn't help. We've had the house closed up for months on Mammie's orders. Well, I thought we had. I don't know how long those two have been coming here. They'd wanted nothing to do with the place until very recently. Aurelia said it was too painful, yet here she is."

I trailed my fingers over the dusty cover on the sofa. "People deal with grief in different ways."

"Maybe Mammie's death changed their minds."

"Or my arrival."

"They'll come around. This could be home for all of you some day."

I shrugged as I looked around and let the memories in. "Yeah, maybe. I don't think any of us are ready for that yet. I think I'm good at the inn."

Addie nodded, then gestured toward the back of the house. "Before we go, then, I thought you should go through some things in your dad's old study. Your mom left it virtually untouched, but maybe there's something there that can help with the inn."

"Like insurance or secret accounts nobody knows about?"

"Who knows? You don't until you look, right?"

I started heading that way. "Yeah, I guess it won't hurt. Well . . . it will, but it's okay."

"While you do that, I'll go see if I can get anything out of Aurelia."

As I entered my father's formal study with its large mahogany desk and many bookshelves, all filled with leather-bound books, I took note of the mixed feelings I had for both of my parents. I was at once angry at them for what they had done to me, to all of us, yet I missed them so much and ached to see them just one more time. I hated and loved them at the same time. I supposed I wasn't the only child who felt that way toward their parents, but it was new to me. A few weeks ago, I'd thought I had no parents, no family at all.

I pulled the covers off the furniture and sat in Daddy's chair and spun it around, taking his office in. Heavy drapes blacked out the windows, and although my vampire eyes could still see, I turned on the desk lamp. After another glance around, I began going through the drawers, finding interesting tidbits here and there. At some point during my rummaging, music began playing again, but not rap and not quite as loud as before. Low enough that I could hear Aurelia and Addie singing and even laughing, and I smiled to myself.

Mom and Mammie must have been through everything, because I didn't find a single item relevant to insurance, bank accounts, or anything of the like that didn't have a copy I'd already seen at the inn. However, I did find some photo albums. I sat on the leather loveseat by the shelves and paged through them, allowing the pictures to begin filling in the holes in my memory. As I studied the photos of the three of us kids growing older, I could see in Aurelia's face what I'd often seen in Aster McCabe's, and a sadness filled me. She'd grown up in my shadow. And then our parents had shipped me off to have a perfect life without them, leaving them here to die and Aurelia and Gabe to pick up the pieces. Because I'd been turned, I hadn't even been able to become the doctor that had been all of our dreams. Tears streamed down my cheeks by the time I closed the back cover.

"No more photos for now," I muttered as I replaced the album on the book shelf and wiped my tears dry.

My gaze fell on one of the leather-bound books that looked to be different from the others. I pulled it off the shelf, and it wasn't a press-printed piece of literature like the others. It was very old, soft, supple leather, tied with a leather strap. I carefully untied it and opened the cover to find yellowed paper with swirly handwriting. I'd found a journal. More specifically, I'd found my mom's journal. Dated in the 1840s.

"Whoa," I breathed as I dropped back into the loveseat.

Turning the delicate pages carefully, I became immersed in Mom's notes of a time long gone by, in a place far away. She wrote about her life in a small village in Romania, the ritual ceremony of when her parents triggered her moroi gene, meeting my father and marrying him. How they'd planned to use their gifts of giving people comfort and setting them at ease combined with manipulating earth and stone to build and run their own inn in Romania. I read about their life together as husband and wife, living near their families, including Luiza, who'd been married to my dad's brother.

And then about the births of four children. One was Madame Luiza's. And the other three were mom's.

"What on earth?" I muttered under my breath as I reread the entries. I looked up, although not really seeing the office around me. "Mom and Dad had previous children. So did Luiza. What happened to them? Did I know about this?"

I don't know how long I sat there wondering about these older siblings we had but was pretty sure we'd never known about. The office was only lit by the lamp, but the light in the hallway had changed. And then I realized how quiet the house had fallen. No music or dancing or laughing or talking. No breathing or heartbeats.

I tied the journal up to protect the pages and hurried into the main part of the house, out to the foyer. Night had fallen while I'd been engrossed in photos and journal entries, moonlight pouring through the soaring windows over the front door. "Addie? Aurelia? Gabe?"

Nobody answered me. Where had they gone? Why had they taken off, leaving me alone? I called for them again. Dead silence.

Then a large shadow swept overhead. I looked up. And screamed.

CHAPTER 11

a white bat hung from the ceiling. A bat the size of a man. I blurred for the front door, but it beat me there, dropping in front of me just as I was about to grab the handle. I jerked my hand back before I touched the hideous monster. It had the body of a man, naked and muscular, with large wings spread out from its outstretched arms to below the knee. Its bald head was also that of a man's, but with pointed ears, sharp-edged cheekbones, and fangs. Its irises were pitch black, but a green light shone in the pupils. Grayish-white, leathery looking skin covered it from head to toe, not a single hair to be seen.

"Like what you see, puppet?" it asked me, and I gasped with surprise that it spoke. *Teased.*

I spun and ran, blurring for the back door. But the thing was faster than me, soaring over me, and swooping me up into talon-like fingers. I kicked and thrashed and tried to wriggle myself free from its hold, but it was so much stronger than me, even with my vampire strength. We crashed through the two-story Palladian windows at the back of the house and immediately climbed higher in the sky, veering to the right to avoid the mountainside. I opened my mouth to scream, but I suddenly felt like a hand had clapped over it, something invisible silencing me. No matter how hard I arched and thrashed, the beast kept its grip, its claws digging into my shoulders as we soared over town. The icy air bit at my face and hands.

Town square passed under us, to our right, and the lights of emergency vehicles sped below, headed in the opposite direction. I tried yelling at them to turn around, but couldn't. The acrid odor of fire and smoke came faint on the air as we traveled away from the source.

We began descending on the far side of town as we approached the east mountain. The thing expertly avoided crashing through the tree branches before coming in for a landing at the back of a log cabin at the end of a cul-de-sac. I knew this house. I'd remembered it one of my first days here, although I hadn't known why then. But now I did. I'd been here many times.

This was the Rocas' home.

The thing released me several feet from the ground, and my feet had barely touched the wooden deck in front of the back door before I lunged for the edge. But a powerful hand grabbed me by the back of the neck and jerked me inside. Another hand gripped my upper arm hard enough to bruise it, and the person behind me shoved me forward, making me stumble. They kept me upright, though, pushing me until I started walking, through the familiar kitchen and headed for the basement door. They practically carried me by the neck and arm down the stairs into the dark cellar, unrelenting regardless of how hard I bucked and kicked, always missing my mark.

A second pair of hands wrapped around my wrists and lifted my arms above my head and out. I snarled and snapped at them, but they remained out of reach. Cold metal replaced the long, bony fingers, clamping around my wrists. The sound of metal grated against metal as my arms were lifted higher until my feet left the ground. More metal cuffed my ankles, and my legs were also pulled apart. I jerked against the bindings to no avail. A bright light was suddenly turned on, momentarily blinding my sensitive eyes. Once they adjusted, I found Mrs. Roca, wearing black dress pants and a yellow silk blouse, standing in front of me, and I was surprised I even recognized her.

I remembered thinking she was beautiful, just as beautiful as my own mom, but that wasn't quite the word I'd use now. She was vamped out—her eyes bloodshot, her skin blanched and veiny looking, her fangs protruding between her lips—but her beauty could still be seen. Only now, her pale skin pulled taut over the sharper edges of her bones. Her lashes weren't as long and thick as they'd been before, something I'd always envied a little of all the Rocas. Her hair wasn't as thick and glossy as I remembered either. Not the jet-black it used to be. What happened to her?

A whimper from the corner beyond her caught my attention. My eyes bugged when they saw my sister and brother chained up just like me on the other side of the room. Blood dripped from Gabe's lower lip, and Aurelia's clothes were shredded. Fear shone in their wide eyes. I thrashed and fought against the metal cuffs, but they only dug in deeper. I tried to scream, but the invisible muffle remained.

A movement to my left brought the man-bat into view as it moved closer to my siblings. I tried to scream and fight again, ignoring the pain of the cuffs bite into my skin. I just needed to get to them, free them before that monster hurt them even more.

"Where's the witch?" Mrs. Roca demanded.

"She wasn't there," the creature said, and before my eyes, its wings disappeared and it morphed into Mr. Roca. Except a thinner, much more muscular and younger Mr. Roca than I remembered. He could almost be mistaken for any of his sons, if not for the glowing irises, now a lime green instead of black.

Mrs. Roca's green eyes narrowed as she glared at me, but spoke to her husband, and as her vamp traits faded, I noted another difference in her. Her eyes used to be grayer. Moroi eyes, as Xandru had said. Now they were a brighter green. Almost as bright as her husband's. "Did Adelaide see you?"

"No. She was gone before I got there," he answered as he pulled a pair of black jeans off a work bench scattered with various tools and, I couldn't help but notice, some mighty long, sharp-looking knives. I immediately averted my eyes to not give away that I'd seen them while I tried to figure out how to break out of these cuffs and reach the knives before they caught me. My vampire abilities were not an advantage with them. *Come on, Kales, think!*

"You damn well better hope so," Mrs. Roca replied to her husband, "or she'll have the Court here in no time. I will not watch them put you down."

Mr. Roca buttoned his jeans, then pulled on a dark gray button-down shirt. He stared at me as he began buttoning it. "Nor I you. We'll take care of this, Isabella. Just like I promised. Now, get the girl."

Aurelia's eyes widened with fear, her body thrashing against the restraints, her cries muffled like mine. I once again tried to fight my way to freedom as Mrs. Roca approached my sister, and tears filled my eyes. But then she passed Aurelia and Gabe and disappeared around a corner, a smirk on her face. *Bitch!*

A moment later she returned, gently leading a young woman about my age dressed in only a satin teddy. Her glassy blue eyes wandered around the room as her finger twirled in a long, blond lock. Mrs. Roca walked over to me and beckoned at the girl.

"Over here, dear," she said with a kind voice, and the blonde followed until she stood in front of me. Mrs. Roca gave me a tight grin. "We brought you a present, *Michaela*." She said it like Mammie had, dropping the hard K. "How long has it been since you've had human blood straight from the vein?"

My eyes widened, and I shook my head. *No!* I tried to scream. It'd been more than two years, when I'd first been turned.

"Come now, dear, just a taste." She placed her hand on the girl's head and tilted it to the side, exposing her throat. The older woman blew across the girl's skin, engulfing me with her delicious scent. My tongue automatically swept over my lips as my gaze fell on her prominent carotid. The throbbing artery called to my thirst.

But I knew what just a taste did. I knew there was no such thing as "just a taste," not when direct from the vein. I'd almost killed last time I'd wanted just a taste of the fresh, warm blood. My mouth watered, and I was nearly panting.

"Here, I'll start," Mrs. Roca said, and she vamped out before bending over the girl's throat and latching on.

The woman flinched but otherwise didn't respond. She was under compulsion.

Mrs. Roca came up and licked the blood off her lips, but left the wound gushing. "Hurry, or I might take her all for myself."

She shoved the woman up against me, her bleeding throat level with my nose and mouth. I turned my head, refusing. Mr. Roca suddenly stood behind me, his large hand on my head, pressing me toward the girl. My lips touched her throat, the deliciousness filled me, and I couldn't help it. *Just a taste*. I licked the warm, thick liquid from my lips, my eyes fell closed, and for a moment, I thought I'd died and gone to heaven. I needed more. *Now*.

I lunged forward with a sudden thirst that felt like fire in my throat. My lips closed over her wound, my fangs sank into her skin to widen it, and I sucked her delicious, sweet and salty life force, my eyes rolling back with bliss.

"That's our girl. Drink up. Then only a couple more to go," Mr. Roca cooed, and at first, the sound was soothing, encouraging, but then something flipped inside me.

I jerked back. *No!*

"Drink!" Mrs. Roca spat as she shoved the girl in my face again. I shook my head violently, refusing. Her eyes glowed green, and she growled at me. Then she went in for the kill herself.

"No, darling," Mr. Roca said as he pulled the blonde out of his wife's embrace as though she were a ragdoll. Mrs. Roca hissed at him, and I thought she was about to pounce. He held up a hand and shook a finger at her. "This one's Michaela's. Remember the plan. You can have yours later. After we take care of this for the kids."

Mrs. Roca growled lowly, but backed off.

"Now come on, Michaela, drink up," he said to me, once again holding the girl in front of me. I pressed my lips together and turned my head. "Well, I'll just leave her right here. You won't be able to resist for long."

He let go of the girl, and she collapsed to the floor. Her eyes fluttered closed as she fell into a deep sleep. Her wound still seeped, and flames licked up my throat at the smell. He eyed me for a long moment.

"Let's have a talk, why don't we?" he said, and he made a gesture in front of me. The strange muffled feeling disappeared. The whimper I couldn't control because of the burn finally could be heard.

"Why are you doing this?" My voice was choked, raspy, as everything within me yearned for the girl at my feet. For her blood. "What did I do to you?"

He laughed, but no humor filled the creepy sound. "You mean, what did you to do *us*. All of us. My whole damn family, if I don't put a stop to it."

"I don't know what you're talking about. I haven't done anything!"

He growled in my face. "You fucking exist!"

I flinched as though he'd slapped me.

"You went and turned yourself when you weren't supposed to, not giving a fuck what you were doing to the rest of us. Not just your family, but mine, too." His facial features began to morph back into the beast. "You did this!"

"I . . . I have no idea what you're talking about."

He glared at me with green eyes. "You're making us go strigoi. That curse on you, on your family—it's ruining us, too. But I won't let it. Mrs. Roca and I will deal with it, but I won't let you get our kids killed by the Court. I'll make sure it's you instead."

"Now drink," Mrs. Roca ordered, gesturing at the woman at my feet.

"I will not."

She laughed. "And you pretend not to understand. You know exactly what will happen."

"Why the hell do you want me to kill her? What did *she* do?"

Mrs. Roca shrugged. "*She* existed. She was convenient, left in one of our cabins while her boyfriend went out skiing. We have him, too. He'll be your next kill."

"What? No!"

"Oh, yes, dear. You will. You will start to go strigoi, the Court will kill you, and this damned curse will be over with. *Before* it takes our children."

"What the fuck is strigoi?" I yelled.

They both fell silent and stared at me. Mrs. Roca tilted her head. "You really don't know?"

I didn't answer, thinking it was pretty damn obvious.

"It's what happens to moroi when they kill one too many humans," Mr. Roca said with a thrill in his voice. "It's what's happening to me, to Mrs. Roca. You saw what I turn into. But that's barely the beginning. Moroi are mortals. Fully turned strigoi are immortal. Stronger, faster, more abilities, indestructible, unstoppable."

"Each kill makes you even thirstier," Mrs. Roca added, and I could hear the thirst in her own voice. "Leaves you burning for the next one until you can't fight it any longer. But each kill stains your soul, until it turns so black, you simply don't care anymore. You become a monster, and not even the Coven can end you."

"Why the *hell* would you want me to be like that?" The thought of becoming what they described scared the shit out of me, but it made no sense.

"We don't," Mr. Roca said, and now I was even more lost. "We just want you on your way to becoming strigoi, where it's too late to turn back. Far enough that the Court has no choice but to put you down before you get out of control."

"Like you are?" I spat.

"I'm not quite there, but will be soon enough," he said with a sickening smile. "Someone fast enough with a blade might still be able to take my head. But I'm not worried about that anymore. The missus and I will be long gone before the Court knows about us. They'll be too focused on you. And once they end you, the curse breaks, and our family won't have to know what this is like."

"What curse?" I asked.

"That's enough questions. Now drink!"

"If you're going to make me do this, you owe me a full explanation. What curse?"

"Tell her," Mrs. Roca said. "It might motivate her, if she cares about her brother and sister at all."

My gaze flew to Aurelia and Gabe hanging by their wrists, watching us. Both of their bodies trembled. I looked back at the Rocas. "Tell. Me."

Mr. Roca rubbed his chin. "The curse against your family after their first offspring went strigoi."

I blinked as I remembered the journal that I'd read just today. I must have dropped it when Mr. Roca's bat-form kidnapped me.

"Nobody knows why, but your older brothers and cousin weren't quite right. Never were. As soon as they were matured, they gave in to the bloodlust. They went on a murderous rampage throughout the countryside back in our Old Country. They killed dozens in only a few nights, trying to quicken the process of becoming strigoi. They *wanted* to be monsters, and they knew if they didn't force the transformation fast enough, they'd only need to be decapitated to be stopped. But if they were fully changed, they thought nothing could stop them. Witches and sorcerers had to be hailed to contain them before they killed any more. It took much magic, but they were eventually eliminated. Your uncle was killed in the mayhem."

I stared open-mouthed as my brain processed all of this. Once it did, I looked over at Aurelia and Gabe. She shook her head. She hadn't known either. Gabe only stared, his eyes glassed over with fear. They shouldn't be hearing this.

"Your parents and your aunt had to pay. Losing their children, and your uncle, wasn't enough. So the magic wielders cursed them."

"Cursed all of us," Mrs. Roca corrected.

Her husband nodded. "Our punishment was minimal. We didn't have children yet, so we'd had no part in the murders. But since the Rocas served the Petrans, the mages said our ties were too close. They cursed all of us to not be able to bear children for seven generations of the families who'd been massacred. And then, if your parents or your aunt had any more children, their moroi genes could not be triggered, or the whole family bloodline would die. They wanted to ensure the intense bloodlust didn't repeat itself."

I squinted at him. "But if the gene's not triggered, they would die anyway."

"The matured eventually would, but not as fast. The curse took them quickly." He nodded toward Aurelia and Gabe. "And the curse takes the *entire* family."

My breath caught. I shook my head. "No. I don't believe you. This has nothing to do with you going strigoi. You're just trying to distract me."

He chuckled. "It really doesn't have anything to do with it, does it? It shouldn't. *We* didn't do anything wrong. But then, shortly after you turned, my brother changed. We had to put him down before the Court found out. Then his wife. And now us. I don't believe in coincidences, Michaela, but when I found out about you, the pieces came together. Your father did this somehow, but I *will* end it. By ending you. Now kill. The. Fucking. *Woman!*"

The blonde flew up off the floor in a blur, and he shoved her in my face again.

"Fuck you!" I spit out.

"She needs motivation," Mrs. Roca said, and in a heartbeat, she stood behind Aurelia, her fangs at my sister's throat.

"No!" I screamed. The metal cuffs tightened on my wrists and ankles, and the chains cranked on their own, pulling me tighter. I fell still. Recalling what Xandru had said, I realized why the Rocas were such good metalworkers. And something else clicked in my mind. My heart squeezed painfully, then shattered into pieces, but I couldn't dwell on that now. I needed to protect my siblings, and I knew what I had to do. "Okay!" I yelled. "Just leave them alone. I'll drink."

"Good answer," Mr. Roca said. "After all, you'll be saving their lives, too. The curse will be lifted from them, as well."

I nodded, sagging with defeat. "I get it. My parents . . . Mammie …" I shook my head as tears spilled. "They died too soon because of me."

"That's right," Mr. Roca soothed. "But you can stop it all. You have the power to protect our children *and* your siblings."

The fear in their faces gave me the motivation the Rocas had hoped for. But not for what they'd expected. As I leaned in toward the girl's bloody throat, I redirected my bloodlust, focusing everything within me on the metal bands wrapped around my wrists and ankles. And it worked. As much as I hated what it meant, I was right. My jaw clenched against the burn, not in my throat now, but on the skin of my extremities as the metal began to melt. The moment I was free, I sprang for Aurelia and Gabe, while retargeting my energy to the knives on the work bench. They flew through the air, one toward Mr. Roca and the other toward his wife.

"What you failed to consider," I seethed, "is that *your* son turned me. And he gave me your power to manipulate metal."

Before they could react, I swished my finger, and the knives sliced across their throats.

I spun and freed Aurelia and Gabe with a simple touch to the metal, releasing the clasps. Wish I'd thought of that when I'd done my own. We ignored the thumps of falling bodies behind us and rushed for the stairs.

To find a whole family of Rocas lined up on them.

CHAPTER 12

Several large bodies and a couple of smaller ones pushed past us as I tried to get Aurelia and Gabe to safety.

"Aw, fuck," a low voice came from behind us.

"Shit," said a girl's voice. "Tase and Xandru were right."

"Go," I urged my sister and brother toward the stairs, needing them gone before shit went bad again. "Get out of here."

"But—" Aurelia looked over her shoulder at me.

"Just go," I hissed, but before I could stop her she turned and threw her arms around me. I gave her a quick return hug, then rushed her and Gabe up the stairs.

They weren't out of sight five seconds when more figures came to the top of the stairs.

"Michaela," Addie gasped as she flew down the steps.

"Are you okay?" Xandru asked me at the same time, his hands on my shoulders, turning me toward him. He raised a hand to my face, but I pulled away.

"Don't touch me," I seethed. "You have no right."

His eyes darkened with confusion.

"Kales, are you okay?" Now Addie turned me around.

I fell into her arms. "I . . . I don't know."

She squeezed me harder. "Well, you will be."

I chuckled humorlessly. "I don't think you've seen that mess over there. I don't think I'll be okay."

She tried to soothe me, but more people came down the stairs. As large as the full basement was, it suddenly felt like an overcrowded tomb.

"What happened down here?" asked a woman dressed in a business suit, her silvery white hair pulled into a fancy twist. A few lines etched her face around her brown eyes as their gaze traveled over the backs of the Rocas gathered around their parents. Then they landed on me. "Michaela?"

As soon as she addressed me, her face clicked in my memory. This was Adelaide's grandmother, Saundra Beaumont, one of the Luna Coven's high council members. One of the most powerful witches in town. The one who both served, and from what I remembered my dad saying, led the Court of the Sun and the Moon. Basically, the person who would decide my fate—if the Rocas didn't first.

"Mr. and Mrs. Roca . . ." Several pairs of eyes suddenly focused in on me. I swallowed the lump in my throat. "They abducted Aurelia and Gabe, and then me."

"Hey, there's a human girl over here," one of the Roca brothers—not Xandru, he still stood there staring at me—said from the place where I'd been shackled. He looked up and tugged on the chains until what was left of the melted cuffs fell in his hands. "What the hell?"

"I think there's a guy somewhere, too," I said. "Another human."

Saundra Beaumont nodded her head to the others behind her, and two began moving about, searching the house. "Why do they have humans here? The girl looks like she's been nearly drained."

"She's alive," another Roca brother said, nearly growled.

"Michaela?" Saundra looked at me again with a white brow raised.

"They wanted me to go strigoi."

Once again, everybody froze and directed their full attention to me. I gave a quick rundown of what had happened, except the part about the curse. I mentioned it and that they believed if I went strigoi it'd be broken, but I said no more about it.

"I don't know if there really was a curse," I said. "Maybe they were just trying to finish the job of framing me for those murders."

Saundra studied me for a moment, probably wondering if she should stay on point or interrogate me about what I knew about the murders.

"It had to have been them," I continued. "I just learned about this strigoi thing, but if they were lying about that, they were definitely *something* different. They would have killed Aurelia and Gabe if they had to. Definitely would have killed that girl and her boyfriend."

"They were definitely going strigoi." One of the Roca brothers strode over to us. Tase, the oldest. He and Xandru exchanged a meaningful look. Addie squirmed next to me. "Their eyes are bright green even in death."

"Tase and I confronted them a couple of weeks ago," Xandru added, "but they denied knowing anything about the first murder. Then there was the second one…" He looked over at me. "We hadn't been able to find either of our parents, though. Until now."

At least now I knew why he'd disappeared right after professing his undying love for me. *Undying* taking on a whole new kind of meaning.

"The curse is truth," Saundra said. "Mihail Petran had come to us years ago, begging for a way to break it. We tried, but we could not find its weak point. There's always a loophole in magic, but this one's is tiny. After you turned, though, something interesting happened with the Rocas. Something that would only happen under a specific circumstance."

"They began going strigoi," I said. "Starting with Mr. Roca's brother."

Saundra nodded. "Yes, and according to Mihail and Irina, that would only happen if someone forced you or your siblings to turn. If someone triggered your gene without your consent, the curse would also jump to that bloodline, but with even more dire consequences."

"That's exactly what happened," I said as my gaze locked with Xandru's. "*Why*, Xandru? Why would you do this?"

"I didn't," he said.

I blew out a breath. "You're going to stand there and flat-out lie to me after all this? Unbelievable!"

"Michaela, please believe me."

"How can I? You admitted to coming to Atlanta. You admitted to wanting more than anything for me to remember you. So you *turned* me? Against my will? And now look what's happened! The repercussions of such selfishness!"

He shook his head while still holding my gaze. "That's not what happened, Kales. I couldn't ever—"

"You killed my parents, Xandru! You killed Mammie! Maybe not directly, but you made it happen. And now *your* parents!"

His whole expression filled with pain. "Michaela—"

I held up my hand and cut him off. "I don't want to hear more lies. Do you know how I knew? Look at those metal cuffs. I did that. It's not the first time I've controlled metal. Where do you think that ability came from, considering it's a *Roca* trait?

All of the Roca siblings reacted at once, filling the room with a loud din.

"Enough," Saundra said with a firmness that hinted at her power, silencing everyone. "We haven't found a way to break the curse, but we do have a way to contain it. To ensure this strigoi business doesn't continue."

I stood up straighter in front of her and lifted my chin. "I'll do it."

She peered at me with Addie on one side of her and her other people gathered behind her. "You don't know what's required."

"I assume you take care of the source of the problem. Me. I'll do it, but not for the Rocas. For Aurelia and Gabe. Whatever it takes to give them some kind of normal life."

She nodded. "You're partially right. It will sever the curse from them. But you're not the true source, are you?"

I swallowed as she looked beyond me at Xandru and the rest of the Rocas.

"We can contain the curse to the one who turned Michaela against her will. The blood thirst will take hold, whether immediately or in weeks or months, we do not know, but it will come, and it will come on strong. Everyone here is aware of what happens when a moroi goes strigoi. It's not tolerated in Havenwood Falls, and we will not allow it to escape our town either. We will end the life before it's transformed into a monster."

The Rocas all burst out in protest, yelling at each other, at me, at Saundra. But then they suddenly fell still and silent as the witches moved around the room and into formation, encircling the family, chanting as they lifted their arms above their heads. My hair began to stand on end as the volume increased and energy sparked in the air. They continued circling, the energy built higher, and the urgency of their words increased. Then they stopped their movement, and each of them pushed their hands toward one of the Roca siblings, then pulled. A green light followed their movements, as though flowing out of the Rocas' bodies. Then they gathered the light above all their heads, swirling in a streak until it tightened and formed into a ball. As the ball began to shrink, my lungs seized.

A sob flew up into my throat, and I clapped my hand over my mouth to hold it in. Reality came crashing down on me. Xandru was about to be given a death sentence. I felt so much anger toward him for all that he'd done, but the thought of him no longer existing in this world . . . it was unfathomable. He was the love of my life. The love that had never truly reached its potential because so much had been against us. And maybe what he did was wrong, but could I blame him? If the situation was reversed, would I have done the same? It's not like he knew about the curse and the consequences. And I'd thought about making Sindi reverse Ryan's compulsion numerous times, and what we had was nothing compared to Xan and me.

My whole body curled inward as the green ball traveled over the group's heads, circling slower and slower as though searching for the one it now belonged to. Xandru had been staring at me the whole time, and I fell into his beautiful gaze now as the ball hovered over his head. Tears streamed down my cheeks.

I love you, I mouthed as the ball wobbled, then dropped.

Everybody gasped. The sob I'd been holding in choked me. *Oh. My. God. Oh my god, oh my god, oh my god. What just happened?*

Addie cried out. "Tase? NO!"

All eyes stared as the green light filled the man standing next to Xandru.

Seconds ticked by in total silence. The light faded, settling into him. Then Addie's sobs broke through as she lunged for Xandru's brother.

"No, no, no," she cried as she held onto him and they fell to the floor. "What the fuck did you do?"

I stood glued to the spot as everyone else seemed to process everything much faster than me. A multitude of emotions battled inside me, and I didn't know how to feel.

But then that big, powerful body moved toward me, those stunning eyes locked on me, and I knew exactly what I felt. I lunged into Xandru's open arms and wrapped my entire body around his. I never wanted to let go. With great reluctance, I eventually pulled back and cradled his face in my hands.

"It wasn't you," I said.

He gave me a small smile. "Don't you understand? More than anything, all I want is for you to live the life *you* want, not what others choose. All I want is for you to be happy. Even if it's without me."

I shook my head as I returned his smile. "It will never be without you."

None of us wanting to stay in the big mansion yet, Aurelia, Gabe, and I walked into the inn, each of them holding my hand. As soon as we passed through the double doors, I gasped, Aurelia screamed, and Gabe simply froze.

"My babies," said the figure standing behind the front desk with a big smile on her face. "Did you miss me?"

"Do you see and hear that?" Aurelia whispered.

"You, too?" I asked.

"Uh-huh."

"How?" Aurelia asked.

"It's Havenwood Falls, dear." The woman moved toward us, eliciting another gasp and a scream. "Nothing makes sense here."

"Oh. My. God. She just walked *through* the fucking desk," Aurelia said.

"Language, love," the ghostly figure warned.

Gabe blanched and began to turn around. "I'm out of here."

"No way," I hissed, clasping his shoulder. "We stick together now. Man up."

"Oh, dear. I didn't mean to frighten you." She clapped her hands under her chin. "I'm just so happy to see you. All of you, together."

"Um . . . I don't mean to be rude," I said, "but, well, we just buried you, Mammie!"

She squealed with delight. "You called me Mammie!"

"It's really you, isn't it?" Aurelia asked. She stepped forward and tried to touch Madame Luiza, but her hand went right through her.

The old woman giggled like a child. "That tickled!"

Whether from giddiness or exhaustion, the three of us all broke down in a fit of laughter. Mammie clapped her hands and danced around us.

"What are you doing here?" I asked, then I frowned. "Are you okay? Are you stuck between planes or something? Does someone need to guide you into the light?"

Mammie laughed. "You have sure come to accept things, haven't you? Even the most bizarre. You must have had an eventful time while I was gone."

"You don't want to know," I muttered. To a ghost. We were talking to a freaking ghost.

"Why *are* you here, Mammie?" Aurelia asked.

"Well, someone has to keep an eye on you kids," she said with a wink. Then she looked at me. "And I thought I could help you out around here."

I cocked my head. "How exactly would you do that?"

"I admit I am no genius when it comes to marketing, but I've watched enough TV. I'm pretty sure haunted hotels tend to stay booked up."

"Mammie! You're a genius!" I threw my arms open, but then dropped them. "I'd hug you, but . . . well . . . this is awkward."

"It's okay, dear. I feel your energy." She smiled. "It's good energy, too. I'm so happy for you. Welcome, home, Michaela."

I grinned back. "It's good to be here."

After the shock of finding a ghost in our lobby wore off, it didn't take long for everyone to settle down for the night. Over the next couple of days, though, we planned how to make the most of Mammie's paranormal visits, as well as brainstormed ideas for the changing season and all of the festivals coming up in the spring and summer. As new guests arrived or townspeople stopped by for one reason or another, Mammie tipped me off as to who was human and who was supernatural, shocking me every time. Well, except for the creepy old dude with shifty eyes who came in. He had weasel-shifter written all over him, and Mammie and I worked together to scare him away.

Addie didn't come by for several days, even after I told her about Mammie, caught up in Coven business. The smoke I'd smelled while in Mr. Roca's clutches had been a fire at the library, which was where she'd disappeared to right before the Rocas kidnapped Aurelia and Gabe. As the Court's business manager and Coven liaison, she was required to monitor the scene for any suspicious supernatural activity. Since then, she and the rest of the Coven and Court have been busy trying to quell rumors about the Rocas and the fire.

Xandru was held away, too, unsurprisingly with family issues. Such as nearly killing his brother for what Tase had done. The police were even called and would have been happy to kill two vampires, especially Rocas. So the brothers made up, but still had much to work out, with their family and each other.

Tonight, however, was ours. We had a date at the Fallview Tavern at the top of the falls. Aurelia helped me get ready for the evening in my cottage before she went to spend the night with her friend Lena. Gabe was already at a friend's house for a sleepover. They were making the most of their last non-school night after their bereavement, and I planned to, as well.

A knock at the door had Aurelia and me exchanging a happy glance. I looked in the full-length mirror one more time.

"You look amazing," my sister appraised, and I felt amazing in the silky black dress and black suede stilettos. I rarely dressed up, because it just wasn't my style, but when I did, I felt all the more beautiful.

"Someone's getting laid tonight," Aurelia sing-songed.

"Shut *up*," I muttered as I headed for the door, sure the vampire ears on the other side heard her.

But they weren't the vampire ears I was expecting. I opened the door to find Addie and Tase on the porch, both looking quite nervous. I stepped outside, rubbing my bare arms against the cold bite of the night that promised another snowstorm. We stood in awkward silence for several beats.

"Um . . . how are you?" I asked Addie, noting the stress and sadness etched into her face.

"Tase has something to tell you."

I looked at him with a brow lifted, mixed emotions swirling within. He'd caused so much heartache for my family and now for his own, but I wasn't sure if a death sentence was quite fair. His forlorn expression tugged at my heart strings.

"I want to apologize," he said as his green gaze, similar to Xandru's but more green than gray now, held mine. "I did it partly for the money, but I didn't know the truth of the consequences."

My brows pinched. "I'm sorry?"

He blew out a sigh. "I was bribed to turn you."

I pulled back and blinked. "By who?"

"It's Coven business," Addie said.

"I think it's *my* business," I countered.

"I promise to tell you when the investigation is final," she replied.

"It was a witch?"

They both nodded.

"She'll be banished," Addie said, "but that's why I can't say who yet."

I nodded. "Fine. But for money, Tase? Really?"

He shoved his fists into his jeans pockets and gnawed on his lip like Xandru did. "Not completely. I thought I was doing Xandru a favor. I went with him on one of his trips to Atlanta, and I saw how fucking miserable he was. The bitch didn't tell me about the curse, so I thought triggering your gene would be a win for everyone—you and Xandru, your family, me. I knew you'd passed the age of maturity, but it was worth a shot. She offered enough money to do the expansions to the ski resort like I wanted, so, well, I did it. I know it sounds like greed. I know it sounds like a Roca thing to do." He looked at Addie and back at me. "But I really was trying to do the right fucking thing for once. Now I'm paying for it."

Addie gave him a look.

"I know. I know. It is what it is," he said. He pulled something out of his back pocket and held an envelope out to me. "I want you to have this. Dad did all kinds of shit to take business from the inn and give it to the resort, and I know you need it."

I took the envelope and looked inside. I held it back out to him. "I can't take this."

"You deserve compensation of some sort."

I shook my head. "It feels too much like blood money."

"Kales," Addie said, "don't be stupid. This goes back to before any blood was spilled. It's money they took from your family. And maybe it'll lead to forgiveness."

"I'm sorry. I can't."

"Think of Aurelia and Gabe."

"We'll be fine. I said I can't take it." I shoved the envelope against Tase's chest. He finally took it back.

"It's okay," he said with a smirk. "The bank note's already been paid off, and you can't give that back."

He turned and walked off, sauntering back to his truck as another drove up the driveway. My body immediately sensed Xandru.

"Jerk," I muttered as I watched Tase's retreating body.

"He's trying to make amends."

"Feeling guilty on his deathbed?" As soon as the words came out, I regretted them. Addie's face looked crestfallen. "I'm sorry. That was mean. Are you holding up okay?"

She shrugged. "As best as I can. Saundra's been trying for years to come up with a way to counter the strigoi transformation. I've been spending every waking minute researching. I'll find a way. I can't lose him, Kales."

I watched as Xandru poured out of his truck and strode toward us, sexy as ever. "I know what you mean." I turned and gave her a hug. "I believe in you, Bratty Addie. Just, you know, don't squander away the time you do have with him."

She nodded against my shoulder before pulling away. "Now you go have a song-worthy time." She winked before traipsing off the porch.

My eyes fixated on Xandru as his large, powerful body climbed the steps, his breath-taking gaze traveling from my head to my feet and very slowly back up, pausing at places that immediately heated. "Mmm . . . you make me want to skip the dinner date part and dive straight into dessert."

"Alexandru Roca," I said with my best Southern drawl picked up from my time in Atlanta, "what kind of lady do you think I am?"

He wrapped one strong arm around me and pulled me up against him. His breath tickled my ear. "You're mine. That's what kind."

I couldn't argue with that. But I did have an addition. "And you're mine."

"Never to be forgotten."

"Never," I breathed before his mouth claimed mine.

WE HOPE you enjoyed this story in the Havenwood Falls series of novellas featuring a variety of supernatural creatures. Keep going for an excerpt of *Old Wounds* by Susan Burdorf. The series is a collaborative effort by multiple authors.

Subscribe to our reader group and receive free stories and more!

IMMERSE YOURSELF IN the world of Havenwood Falls and stay up to date on news and announcements at www.HavenwoodFalls.com. Join our reader group, Havenwood Falls Book Club, on Facebook at https://www.facebook.com/groups/HavenwoodFallsBookClub/

ABOUT THE AUTHOR

Kristie Cook is a lifelong, award-winning writer in various genres, primarily New Adult paranormal romance and contemporary fantasy. Her internationally bestselling Soul Savers Series includes seven books, as well as several companion novellas. Over 1.2 million Soul Savers books have been downloaded, hitting Amazon's, B&N.com's, and Apple's Top 100 Paid lists.

She has also written The Book of Phoenix trilogy, a New Adult paranormal romance series that includes The Space Between, The Space Beyond, and The Space Within. The full trilogy is available now.

Besides writing, Kristie enjoys reading, cooking, traveling, getting her hippie on, and feeding her addictions to coffee, chocolate, cheese, The Walking Dead, Game of Thrones, and Supernatural. She has lived in ten states, but currently calls Florida home.

Email: kristie@kristiecook.com
Author's Website & Blog: http://www.KristieCook.com
Facebook: http://www.facebook.com/AuthorKristieCook
Twitter: http://twitter.com/kristiecookauth
Goodreads: https://www.goodreads.com/KristieCook
Instagram: http://instagram.com/kristiecookauth

ACKNOWLEDGMENTS

Thank you to my Maker who stayed with me always, even when my faith wobbled and wavered.

Thank you to my sons, Zakary, Austin, and Nathan, for all that you have taught me about unconditional love and family bonds.

And a very special thank you to all of you who never gave up on me—my parents, my aunt, my writer friends, my readers—even when nobody would blame you if you did.

This collaborative world started as a flicker in my mind several years ago, and finally grew into something more over the last several months. I didn't know exactly what it would become—and I still don't—but I believe wholeheartedly in the idea and its purpose. It could not have happened without the help and support of my aunt and uncle, and the insight and wisdom of Meredith Frank Mendez, the intellectual property attorney who took the time to understand what I wanted to accomplish and created a contract that could make that happen. I also give a shout-out to my Dynamis sisters, Kallie Ross, Morgan Wylie, and Lila Felix, for giving me feedback and cheering me on when I began throwing out this crazy idea. Also to Rick & Amy Miles and their Red Coat PR team, who have been great supporters of me as a writer, as a friend, and as a publisher. And to my betas, Julie Bromley and Stacey Nixon; and to Liz Ferry at Per Se Editing for making my words shine.

Finally, I thank the creative souls so far involved in this constantly growing and evolving project. Regina Wamba, Art Director, and the authors who've created the characters and settings of Havenwood Falls: Susan Burdorf, E.J. Fechenda, Kallie Ross, Morgan Wylie, Kristen Yard, T.V. Hahn, Amy Hale, Lila Felix, R.K. Ryals, Michele G. Miller, Belinda Boring, and Stacey Rourke. You've made this project everything I dreamed it would be and so much more. I can't wait to see what happens next!

Old Wounds (A Havenwood Falls Novella) by Susan Burdorf

Betrayed by love, Sherry Grimes flees the city, seeking solace in an unfamiliar place that calls to her from deep in the mountains. But her search for comfort goes awry when she's chased by a wolf through the forest, falls, and blacks out. She awakens in a strange room with a mysterious and forbidding—yet undeniably sexy—man by her side. So much for finding solitude. But despite the craziness that brings her to the small eccentric town, she discovers herself drawn into the magic that is Havenwood Falls.

Russell Higgins had long ago given up the idea of finding the one he could trust his secrets to—until he met Sherry. One look at the feisty woman with a broken heart has him defying his pack and rethinking his own ideas of his perfect mate. What he can't deny is the wolf inside, claiming the human as his.

Bradley Monahan wants Sherry back, and he would do anything to make that happen. Even fight the mysteries of a town that doesn't forgive transgressions.

While love may heal old wounds, it's the fresh ones that Sherry must overcome to find her way back home. Wherever that may be.

OLD WOUNDS

AN EXCERPT

Sherry threw her Ford Focus into gear, wishing she was driving Brad's Viper instead of her old clunker. She ignored the vehicle's hesitation and the grinding sounds that came from underneath as she sped backwards out of the driveway without looking. Banging into the garbage can, she winced, knowing the heavy rubber container likely dented the side of the car, but not really caring.

She just needed to be gone, and to be gone as quickly as possible. As she spun the car to face the other end of the cul-de-sac, momentarily stopping to shift gears once more, Brad ran up and pounded on the window, startling her. He was bare-chested, his ripped muscles bulging with effort as he tried to force her to look at him. He wore a pair of gray sweatpants and little else. Normally the sight of his hard, athletic body would cause her to pause and stare at him with hunger, but today she only felt disgust and anger.

"Sherry, come on!" Brad's muted plea came through the closed window. Her fiancé—correction, *former* fiancé—raced barefoot alongside the slowly moving vehicle as she attempted to leave. He had one hand on the locked door handle and the other on the window as he tried to keep her from moving forward.

Sherry's heart beat out a rhythm that begged her to flatten him, but she waited for him to retreat back a step before she glared at him.

Rolling down the window, she said, "Get away from the car, or I'm gonna run over your toes."

Brad wisely stepped farther back, hands raised in surrender. His face turned a bright shade of red. He tossed his black hair out of his eyes. Pointing a finger at her, he said, "Go ahead, run off like a baby. You never were a good lay. I don't need you anyway."

"You will when the rent comes due next week," Sherry spat out before she sped off down the street. In the rearview mirror, which Sherry mentally kicked herself for looking into, she saw the blonde draped around him, rubbing his chest and consoling him in the only way a strumpet like her knew how to.

The girl was dressed in the silk robe Brad had given Sherry on her last birthday. Her favorite silk robe. The one Brad said brought out the blue in her eyes and the sexy in her toned and petite body. She was half-tempted to whip the car around and rip the silk off the woman's slender, tanned form, but decided to forgo that pleasure in favor of getting the heck away from there. Flipping her dark hair over her shoulders, she forced herself to keep her eyes on the road.

A short while later, blinded by tears, she nearly sideswiped a delivery truck and city bus before her pounding heart calmed down and she could breathe normally again. After several hours, with the radio blasting rock music loud enough to melt her eardrums, Sherry pulled over to the side of the road into a small rest area. She had no idea where she was, or where she was going, but something had told her to keep driving, so she followed her gut instinct.

The brisk spring air, chilled with the promise of more winter this close to the mountains of Colorado, greeted her as she emerged from the car. Stepping into a slushy puddle, she groaned in frustration. These were her favorite black heels, their leather now ruined forever in the salty, half-melted snow that encased her foot up to the ankle.

Sherry grabbed her cape from the passenger side and wrapped the thin material around her cream-colored silk blouse. Neither article of clothing was any protection from the cold air that whipped around her. Her dark hair had fallen from the loose bun she'd put it in earlier while driving to keep it out of her eyes. She shivered.

The sound of laughter drew her eyes to a family walking toward the entrance to the building that housed the bathrooms and snack machines. The little girl held tightly to her father's hand, while the boy—in his mother's arms as he was just a toddler—hugged the woman tightly. Looking over her shoulder at her husband who walked slightly behind them, the woman smiled at something he'd said with a look of complete adoration, which he returned with an easy smile of his own, and Sherry felt her throat tighten in jealousy.

Would she ever see anyone look at her like that?

She'd thought Brad would be that one, the one who would make her heart sing with passion that could last forever, but he obviously played their love song out of tune. What was so wrong with her that she couldn't find anyone to love her for longer than it took to cash her paycheck?

She'd met Brad in church, for Christ's sake. How could he have turned out to be such a snake? Was this bimbo the first, as he'd claimed while throwing on his pants to chase after her when she fled? Or was this one just the first he'd been caught with? If she hadn't come home from work early today due to a gas leak near the therapy office at the middle school, she never would have known anything about what he was up to when she was gone each day. Who knows how long this had been going on without her knowledge? Brad certainly wasn't going to tell her, and the bimbo was barely able to string a sentence together, so no help there.

Shivering in the cold, Sherry already regretted her hasty decision to run away. She should have made him, and the bimbo, of course, leave. She considered turning around and driving home, but the last thing she wanted to do was have another argument with him or, worse yet, admit she was wrong to leave so quickly. Even though she knew she wasn't.

That love nest of his was *her* apartment, dammit. She should have made *him* leave. Her face darkened as she remembered the sounds that greeted her when she'd opened the door, sounds she was all too familiar with making herself after a few glasses of good wine and great jazz.

Pinching her lips, she closed her eyes, willing the tears not to fall.

"Lady?" said a small voice to her right. "Are you okay? Do you need a sucker?"

Slowly opening her eyes, Sherry said, "No, thank you." Under her breath she muttered, "I *am* the sucker," which came out louder than she intended.

Sherry looked down to see a tiny blonde girl holding up a bright red sucker, the kind the dentist used to give her back when she was young, if she was a good girl and didn't squirm too much in the seat while they drilled her teeth. She'd always thought it ironic that a dentist would give sugar on a stick to a kid whose teeth he'd just worked on, but she hadn't complained too loudly. And it *had* seemed to ease the pain, at least for a little while.

"Thank you," Sherry said, reconsidering. She took the sucker the little girl offered and smiled, hoping her mouth made the appropriate shape and wouldn't scare the child. Sherry wasn't sure what to do next, as the girl didn't seem to want to leave.

"I am so sorry. I hope Destiny wasn't bothering you too much." The little girl's mother took her daughter by the hand and gently tugged her away.

Sherry smiled crookedly. "Destiny? Perfect name for the first person I speak to right after the disaster of my current life. Almost like a sign."

A sign? Of course it was a sign. Sherry was a firm believer that if you stood still long enough, the universe would find a way to connect with you. Watching the tiny girl and her mother walk with hands clasped tightly, she wasn't surprised when the girl turned, locked eyes with her, and gave Sherry a solemn wink before getting in the car with her family and driving off.

Sherry entered, then stood in the middle of the information building as she looked around. She was surrounded by maps marking the nearest hiking trails, along with brochures advertising tourist traps, which were neatly lined up on the wall in metal racks. The slick, curved, white walls and cheap marble flooring somehow both soothed and unsettled her. Sherry felt the walls closing in on her, although nothing was moving. She felt something happening—changing—inside her. She breathed deeply, eyes closed, and waited to see if the universe had another sign for her.

But nothing came. At least not right away.

No one said, "Go home, patch things up with your skanky boyfriend, and forget that he tends to like other women once in a while." Conversely, nothing else said, "Forget that jerk, keep driving."

Then she heard the soft *swish-swish* of leather-soled shoes on the floor.

"Can I help you, miss?" A kind dark-skinned man, with eyes like chips of coal in his lined and weathered face, looked at her in concern. "Are you lost?" He wore a dark green uniform with a slim silver badge that announced him as BRAD.

Sherry wanted to laugh out loud at the irony of meeting someone with her ex-boyfriend's name, but swallowed back the mirthless sound instead. Sometimes the universe could be cruel. She shook her head, but her watery eyes gave away her true emotional state. The man patted her arm and then squeezed it as he led her over to where the brightly colored and labeled maps rested.

"Perhaps you're looking for a nice place to visit?"

Sherry felt herself gently propelled closer toward the maps. She took the one he proffered to her, barely glancing at it. The second she touched it, she felt a tingle, gentle and insistent, travel up her arm. Nothing uncomfortable or painful—it was more like the pins-and-needles feeling when your arm fell asleep after resting your head on it for a while.

"This is a brochure for a lovely town not far from here called Havenwood Falls. A lot of folks find the town quite pleasant to visit, and I'm sure you will, too."

Sherry raised an eyebrow as she looked at the one-page, double-sided flyer he'd handed to her. The old man stood in front of her, slightly stooped and expectant, as if her decision mattered a great deal to him.

Sherry's eye was caught by the promise of a "cabin in paradise," and she was sold before she even knew what else to say.

Chuckling as if he knew the answer before he asked, the old man said, "You have a plan now?"

"Why, yes," Sherry said, answering his twinkling eyes with a shy smile of her own. "I think I do. These cabins sound wonderful. I see a number down here. I'm going to call and see if they have anything available."

"Good idea. You'd better move on now. There's a storm heading this way soon, and it wouldn't do to get caught in it. Those late spring squalls can be quite temperamental in the mountains. Oh, and miss," the old man said as she started to turn away, "the town is a bit difficult to find. You can take the shuttle outside, or if you prefer to drive your own vehicle, you are welcome to follow the bus for the best way to get there. I strongly urge you to do that. The shuttle bus will be leaving in about ten minutes, though, so you'd better hurry."

Sherry looked where he pointed and saw a large bus idling in the section reserved for buses and trucks to park. She couldn't see through the tinted windows, so wasn't sure if it was full already or not. Since there was so little time to get on the bus if she wanted to take it, and since she was planning to rent a cabin and would need her car, she decided not to take the bus. But she would definitely follow it. She had a feeling the old man was not lying about it being a difficult town to find and wondered why. Mountain roads could be tricky sometimes, with quick turns and perhaps that was the reason why. Either way, she was getting excited at the thought of having a plan.

Sherry nodded. Chuckling once she walked outside, she grinned at the kindness of the old man. He'd been pushy, but pretty darn cute in spite of it. She liked him. Looking back through the glass doors, she was surprised not to see him standing in the doorway watching her. Instead, she could make out a tall, stocky woman behind the desk, shuffling papers and talking to an elderly couple who had just walked up.

After calling the number on the flyer, Sherry was relieved to find there was one cabin left. Because it was higher up on the mountain than she would have liked, she hesitated before committing to the idea of the cabin. *I'm just planning to hike the area for a few days until things have a little time to cool off at home,* she reasoned, justifying both the expense and the remoteness of the cabin.

"That will be three hundred dollars for the week," the woman on the other end of the line said.

Sherry gasped in surprise. "Are you sure? That seems pretty cheap."

"Oh yes, ma'am. Your cabin is very rustic, therefore a little cheaper," the woman replied. Her voice sounded pleasant and certain, exactly the way a customer service person should sound.

Sherry gave the woman her card number and then, just as the woman hung up, thought of a question she needed to ask. When she tried to call back, the number was busy. Hanging up, Sherry decided to go back inside and thank the old man for his help and try the number later.

Moving inside, Sherry waited a minute until the woman behind the counter was free. Sheila's name badge was slightly crooked and not as shiny, but still lettered the same. When Sheila looked up, Sherry smiled sweetly and said, "I wonder if you might give that sweet old guy, Brad, a message for me?"

"Brad?" Sheila's expression was puzzled and annoyed, like she had plenty of better things to do than play secretary.

"Yes, the nice man who helped me a few minutes ago."

"How did he help you?" the woman asked. Her expression had changed from annoyed to cautious, as if afraid of what Sherry might answer.

"Well, he gave me this flyer, the one about Havenwood Falls and renting a cabin. Let him know that's what I've decided to do. And I owe it all to him. So please, tell him thank you."

Sheila hesitated. Biting her lip, she folded her hands together on the desk and stared Sherry squarely in the face. "I'm not sure what game you are playing at here, young lady, but we have no one working here named Brad. And I have never heard of Havenwood Falls. What are you trying to pull?"

Sherry, totally shocked by the woman's attitude—which she felt was totally uncalled for and very hostile—stepped away from the desk. Holding the flyer in front of her, she spoke slowly as if making sure the woman behind the desk would understand the words she was saying. "I just met one of your employees, a nice old man named Brad—it said so on his badge—and he recommended I check into a cabin listed on this flyer."

Sherry flashed the flyer in front of the other woman's face for emphasis and was shocked to discover it did not say "Havenwood Falls" in bold black lettering, but instead encouraged visitors to visit a ghost town about forty miles down the road in the opposite direction.

"Whhhhat???" Sherry dropped the flyer on the desk as if it burned her hand, her face bright pink, and slowly backed away as a young man wearing a backpack walked up to the desk for assistance.

Sherry practically ran from the building and jumped in the car, not surprised to see her hands shaking. *What is going on? I know I had the flyer for Havenwood Falls in my hand. How else could I have called that place for a cabin? Now how will I ever find my way there?*

Sherry looked over at the passenger side of the car, and her eyes widened in shock. On the seat next to her lay the flyer she was sure she'd just dropped on the counter in front of Sheila. And there, written in bold black print, were the words, "HAVENWOOD FALLS. DISCOVER THE MAGIC."

What an odd town motto, she thought as she set the GPS for the location of the cabin rental office where the woman had said they would leave her a key.

"Strange," she said as she tapped the GPS. "What is wrong with this thing? Why won't it pull up the address?"

Sherry shook the device, but nothing changed. She turned it off, and then on again, and still nothing changed. The address was not pulling up at all.

"Now what?" Sherry slumped back in the seat, trying not to cry. This was just too much.

Ahead of her she saw the large bus pulling away from its parking spot. On the side of the bus were the words Havenwood Falls in large lettering with picturesque scenes of the mountains. Without thinking about it too much, Sherry decided she would have to follow the bus like the old man suggested. It looked like the kind of bus you might charter, the kind tourists would use.

Putting the car in gear, once again ignoring the grinding sound, she backed slowly out of her parking spot and pointed the nose of the car toward the highway. Something weird was going on, and she felt like she was in an episode of The Twilight Zone, one of her favorite shows. The grainy black-and-white program had been a staple in her household, much preferred over the banal sitcoms that passed for quality television these days.

As she drove, her phone buzzed, a bright blue-white light signaling an incoming call. She'd turned the ringer off earlier to avoid Brad's many attempts to contact her, so she heard nothing but the buzzing.

Humming to a song on the radio as she ignored the phone, she focused on the road ahead of her. Keeping the bus in sight was pretty easy, since it was so large. She felt the excitement building at the prospect of spending time alone. This was the start of a great adventure. There was no doubt of that in her mind.

Sherry hoped there was a town along the way with a store where she could purchase some clothing appropriate for an extended stay in a cabin, or that the town would be able to supply her with what she needed. She was certain her hastily packed suitcase had nothing she could wear in the woods, and she would need to purchase some food, too. The rumbling of her stomach was a reminder she hadn't eaten in several hours, and the trauma of her situation was starting to take its toll on her. She was starving.

As she drove, she caught sight of a sign on the side of the road noting that Havenwood Falls was just six miles down the road. Not understanding why, she felt almost giddy at the prospect of spending time in the mountains near what she was sure would be a quaint tourist town, if the flyer was a truthful representation of its appearance, that is. After nearly six hours on the road, she was ready to stop for the night. She didn't realize how far this place was from Albuquerque until she glanced at her phone. But she didn't regret one minute of the drive. It had been beautiful driving through the mountains. She hadn't been this spontaneous in years, and it felt good to be free. She hadn't realized how being with Brad had held her back from doing things she enjoyed. He hated the woods, bugs were not his friends, and he swelled up like a dirigible anytime he got bit by something as inconsequential as a mosquito.

She chuckled as she remembered his reaction the one time she'd suggested going weekend camping. He'd just about fainted at the thought of his model-perfect body deformed by nature, a place he referred to as "Alcatraz with trees," since he felt imprisoned if not near civilization, otherwise known as his local craft-beer brewery. "The only nature I ever want to be in, baby," he'd said in perfect seriousness, "is the kind where they have an infinity pool and girls in skimpy white outfits bringing you those drinks with umbrellas in them."

She'd thought he was adorable then. She knew the truth now.

But she'd gone along with it, feeling that being in love meant making sacrifices so the other would feel appreciated. Now she wondered what he'd ever given up for her. She couldn't think of a single thing he'd sacrificed for her good. It had always been her doing the compromising.

She pinched her lips tightly as she thanked her lucky stars they hadn't married yet. It was bad enough imagining the untangling they would have to do when it came time for him to leave now. A marriage would have meant a split of everything right down the middle, and she had a lot of memories tied up in the things in her apartment, not something she was willing to share with someone who treated her so badly. There were photo albums and valuable pieces of decorative art and small treasures that had belonged to her now-deceased parents. Most of the items had been in her family for a long time, and she was not willing to let him take anything just because he'd warmed her bed for a while.

Sherry attempted the phone number once more and sighed in frustration when there was no answer. She paused a moment, considering her options. Should she go forward, or back? Thinking of Brad, his expression smug and sure of himself if she went back, she pinched her lips and decided back was not a place on her GPS. She would only be able to go forward. So, Havenwood Falls it would be. She hoped the old man was right, that she would find in Havenwood Falls the answer to her prayers.

"Yep," she said softly. "This might turn out to be the stupidest idea I have ever had, but—" She paused as the bus increased the distance between them and she stepped on the accelerator to keep it in sight. "Havenwood Falls sounds like exactly what I need right now."

PURCHASE *OLD WOUNDS* at your favorite book retailer.